"I'll never forgive you! I'll hate you till the day I die!"

His nostrils flared as he took a sharp breath. "Never is a long time. You may yet have cause to thank me!"

It took every ounce of control she had not to leap at him and claw him to shreds. It was a measure of just how much passion he could induce in her. The minute she lost her cool, he would have won. That had to be avoided at all costs. She responded instinctively. "For what? Killing my grandfather?"

AMANDA BROWNING is a British author who was born and brought up in Essex, where she still lives. She has had a passion for books since she was a small child and she worked as a librarian before becoming a full-time writer. When she's not reading or writing she loves doing quizzes and embroidery. Her lively contemporary writing style appeals to readers everywhere.

Books by Amanda Browning

HARLEQUIN PRESENTS
1566—A TIME FOR LOVE
1677—AN OLD ENCHANTMENT

AMANDA BROWNING

Savage Destiny

Harlequin Books

TORONTO • NEW YORK • LONDON
AMSTERDAM • PARIS • SYDNEY • HAMBURG
STOCKHOLM • ATHENS • TOKYO • MILAN
MADRID • WARSAW • BUDAPEST • AUCKLAND

ISBN 0-373-11724-8

SAVAGE DESTINY

Copyright © 1993 by Amanda Browning.

First North American Publication 1995.

Printed in U.S.A.

CHAPTER ONE

ALIX PETRAKOS stepped down carefully from the taxi and took a much needed moment to square her shoulders before mounting the flight of steps to the door of the floodlit hotel. There was a supper dance in progress, and, although on another occasion she would have been looking forward to it, tonight it was not her idea of fun. She was tired to her bones. It had been a particularly long and fruitless day after a deluge of long, fruitless days, and had not keeping up appearances demanded that she attend this glittering charity function she would have stayed at home.

An attendant relieved her of her coat, and she took a deep breath before heading for the ballroom, a tall, slim figure who could have stepped right out of the pages of a fashion magazine. Yet, although her evening dress was a St Laurent original, her shoes handmade Italian and her jewellery courtesy of Cartier, Alix knew their days were numbered. Unless she could find the financial backing the family business needed so desperately, everything would have to go. Not that it would be a particularly unpleasant sacrifice, for she was not too enamoured of high fashion and the class structure it implied. No, the sad thing was that collectively the family possessions would do no more than dent the mountain of debts.

Pausing just inside the doorway, she surveyed the crowded room, not surprised to find that she recognised

many of the faces there. Had, in fact, spent long hours
these last few weeks talking to them across desks of every
shape and size. Now, those who witnessed her arrival
were quick to move away, and equally quick to pass on
the news of her family's financial straits in lowered
voices.

It brought a tightness to her lips that sat uncomfortably on her delicate face, which was fine to the point
of fragility—an aspect shown up by the new stylish cut
of her hair, the platinum-blonde crop tapered to her
nape, suiting her perfectly, yet making her grey eyes look
huge and her neck vulnerable. A fact which was unknown to her as she walked inside with all the sang-froid
she could muster.

Helping herself to a glass of wine, she acknowledged
the greetings of those still brave enough to meet her eyes
with a faintly cynical smile. Six months ago it had been
oh, so different. Everything had. Now the façade had
slipped and she had to cope with the consequences of
her father's ill-advised actions. Yet, no matter what these
people thought, she would never have the bad manners
to importune them here.

'Don't look so surprised,' a voice declared mockingly
from beside her. 'When you set out on a collision course
with the rocks, it's a time-honoured tradition for the rats
to leave the sinking ship.'

The low, vibrant tones strummed her nerves, and for
one stomach-lurching moment Alix felt the room actually swim around her. Then her blood froze and her
muscles tensed, and it seemed to take every ounce of her
strength to turn her head to face the voice's owner...
because she knew whom she would see.

'Leaving room for the vultures to swoop down and pick over the rotting carcass,' she riposted swiftly, amazed at how steady her voice sounded, when the sight of the man who had come silently to stand beside her set her heart thudding sickly. 'Why do I get the feeling that to say "fancy seeing you here" would hardly be apt? Sharks can smell blood from miles away, I hear,' she added, not caring if she mixed her metaphors or not. Her mind held only one question: what was he doing here?

Pierce Martineau, as handsome as the devil, and just as black-hearted, afforded her a long lazy smile. 'You've developed claws, Alix, which doesn't surprise me, but, just like a kitten, you've yet to learn when it's wise to scratch.'

The irony stung, reminding her just how weaponless she had once been. Yet those days were long gone. She had developed a wall of defences inches thick. 'As far as I'm concerned, it's always open season on Martineaus!' She allowed her scorn to show, wanting to wither him on the spot. She was reeling with shock. He never came to England. Never.

One black brow shot up. 'Do you always greet an old acquaintance with guns blazing? I'll admit it has novelty value, but it might be wiser to put up your weapon, Alix. These days the enemy doesn't obligingly wear a black hat. For all you know, you could be firing on an ally,' he advised her mildly.

'Ally!' The word came out thick with revulsion. 'You were never that, and never could be. You're the enemy, Pierce, and as such I have nothing but contempt for you,' Alix declared vehemently. Lord, she should have known he would say such a thing. It seemed he had developed a selective memory, while hers remained clear-cut. 'Now I'm afraid you'll have to excuse me. You see, I've become rather more discriminating about the company I keep these days.' With which statement she pointedly turned her back on him and walked away on legs which threatened to give way beneath her at every step.

She had no clear idea where she was heading, just kept on walking until eventually she found herself in a small ante-room from which there was no other exit. She stopped then, discovering she was shaking in every limb. Dear God, why had he had to be here? Hadn't he done enough? Did he need to crow over the remains? She hated him. Hated him as much as she had once loved him; with a depth of emotion that knew no bounds.

Alix bowed her head, her stomach twisting into a painful knot. Pierce Martineau still had everything going for him, possessing the sort of looks that set women's hearts fluttering madly. Once, her own had taken wing in the space of a single beat. She hadn't been immune to the thick glossy blue-black hair and the penetrating blue eyes either, nor the darkly shadowed cheeks framing that beautifully sensuous mouth. His masculinity and self-assurance had shone like a beacon, drawing her, like many another moth, to dance in its dangerous heat and brilliance. He had wined her and dined her, treating her like something beloved and precious, pursuing her with an ardour which had telegraphed to her lovesick heart that he loved her too.

Bitterness was like gall on her tongue, and unconsciously her hand tightened on the glass she still held until her knuckles grew white. He had turned that love to hate with his lies. For it had all been lies! All of it, from start to finish! The angry memory was punctuated by the

sharp crack of glass, instantly followed by her soft cry of pain. The broken glass toppled from her hand, and she stared down blankly at the swift swell of blood on her palm.

It was only then that she realised she was not alone.

'Sweet heaven! Did you cut yourself? Let me look.' Pierce must have followed her, and now he advanced on her swiftly, taking her hand and examining it before she had the chance to pull away.

Alix shuddered, suddenly finding herself staring at his bent head. The lush waves of black hair brought back memories, ones she'd thought safely buried, of how it had felt to the touch. She breathed in sharply, only to have her senses bombarded by the tangy scent of his cologne and the heat coming off him. Then, as if to add insult to injury, his touch sent something close to an electric shock up her arm. Horrified by this totally un-expected and unwanted reaction, she froze in disarray, mind crying out a silent, No!

'You'll live.'

Pierce's declaration snapped her out of her state of shock, and the momentary delay in his looking up gave her just enough time to regain control of her features, leaving them once more remote.

'It's little more than a scratch, and looks clean enough,' he observed, meeting her eyes with a feral glitter in his own. 'What did you imagine the glass was, my throat?'

Try as she might, she could not quite sustain that gaze, and she hastily glanced away from the mockery in those deep blue chasms. Her eyes fell on her hand, and she discovered he had made a makeshift bandage out of his handkerchief. There were traces of scarlet on the pristine white cloth. Her blood. Always her blood when Pierce came into her life! Her lips thinned, that moment of awareness evaporating in the bleak, chill winds of memory.

'If any man deserves to have his throat cut, you do,' she declared coldly, as she glanced up once more, her precious defences safely intact.

If she was scoring any hits, she would never know. Pierce's only reaction was to laugh lightly, at what must seem to him a minnow turning on a pike. 'Many have tried; none succeeds.'

Alix smiled thinly at his supreme conceit. 'Such pride is bound to be brought down. I only hope I'm there to see it.'

There was a moment when something which could have been regret flickered in his eyes, but it was gone before she could quite pin it down. 'That's our heritage in us. Wouldn't you say this has all the makings of a classic Greek tragedy? Vengeful wife plots husband's downfall. Would you dance on my grave, Alix?'

He was toying with her, but she refused to play his game. 'Ex-wife,' she pointed out swiftly, even as her heart contracted sharply—though precisely from what emotion even she couldn't have said at that moment.

Pierce inclined his head in wry acknowledgement, as if he had expected no other answer. 'You say that with such alacrity.'

Her chin came up instantly, and her eyes shot sparks. 'It was the happiest day of my life!'

If she had hoped to wound him, her aim was glaringly abroad. 'Strange, I seem to remember you said the same of our wedding-day,' he reminded her dulcetly, the low timbre of his voice exploding on her senses like dark chocolate, eminently seductive.

To have to acknowledge how he could make her react even now made Alix furiously angry—with herself as much as him for bringing back all too clearly that worst of times.

'I didn't know then what an utter bastard you were.' But she had learnt. How she had learnt.

It seemed he did have a few chinks in his armour, for all trace of amusement left him abruptly. The only movement on his tight face was the tic of a muscle in his jaw. 'It had to be done. You should understand that.'

Grey eyes, darkened by seething emotions, sent him a message of hate. 'I'll never understand it, and I'll never forgive it! I'll hate you till the day I die!'

Nostrils flared as he took a sharp breath. 'Never is a long time. You may yet have cause to thank me.'

It took every ounce of control she had not to leap at him and claw him to shreds. It was a distressing measure of just how he was getting to her. The minute she lost control, he would have won. That had to be avoided at all costs. She responded instinctively. 'For what? Killing my grandfather?'

Her barb found a tender spot, for Pierce took an angry step towards her, then controlled himself with patent effort. 'That you will not lay on me, Alix. He was an old man, I agree, but he lived several years after I last met him,' he pointed out grittily.

Her lips trembled, as much with anger as distress, and she pressed them together. 'Maybe so, but you hastened him into his grave by taking away everything that was precious to him.'

He stiffened in outraged pride, blue eyes becoming flinty, almost dead. 'I took nothing that wasn't mine by right, and in exchange I left him you.'

Alix laughed hollowly. He had left a shell—the carapace of a woman he'd all but destroyed! 'You're a thief and a murderer, and I despise you.'

His face could have been carved from stone, so still did it become. 'Despise away, but I still have something you want.'

'I'd cut off my hand before I accepted anything from you, Pierce Martineau!'

The smile returned, but it was cold, mirthless. 'Always so dramatic. I'd forgotten just what a passionate creature you were, in bed and out of it.'

Only he would have the gall to remind her of her un-inhibited response to him, a response he had used to his own ends. She had been a fool then, but never again. 'You're right, I do have something for which to thank you—for teaching me a valuable lesson. One I'll never forget,' she declared tersely.

There was a fraction of a second before he replied, when his eyes lazily roved over all he could see. The inspection brought a soft curve to his lips, even as it set her back up.

'If I was a good teacher, then you were a very willing pupil,' he said softly, deliberately misinterpreting her. 'You seem to have done well on it too. You're looking even more beautiful than I remember.'

Alix ground her teeth in fury. The fact that he had taken a virgin bride to his bed and awoken her to the pleasures of the flesh was something she found hard to live with, when linked to what had followed. That he should have the insensitivity to remind her of it now churned her stomach. 'I hope you don't expect me to thank you for the compliment, because, quite frankly, the words would choke me!' she shot back.

His eyes danced 'And that would never do. Perhaps I should stop before you have an apoplectic fit, but I can't resist it. I like your hair cut short this way. It makes you look elegant and fragile at the same time. Quite a feat. When did you have it done?' he went on conversationally, and she swallowed down hard on her anger because it was doing her no good, and only appeared to amuse him.

Yet she couldn't help shooting him a challenging look. 'Actually, I first had it cut five years ago!' she retorted, and let him make what he liked of it.

Pierce had never been slow on the uptake, and now he understood immediately. 'Hmm, off with the old, on with the new? I used to be fascinated by your long platinum locks. I'd dream of catching my fingers in it as I made love to you.'

She very nearly choked then, because she had had virtually the same dreams about him, and long after the marriage had ended. Now the memory set like ice about her heart. 'Precisely the reason I had it cut. I wanted nothing to remind me of you,' she added, trying to cut him down to size.

Pierce crossed his arms, regarding her mockingly. 'Yet you haven't forgotten me, it seems. Is that why you're here alone tonight?'

She breathed in sharply. There was no other man like Pierce for asking questions with subtle nuances others missed. 'You can rid yourself of the notion that you have any bearing on my life right now! I'm here alone because my father, as you probably know very well, is ill.

We would have come as a family group, but instead I came on my own. Does that satisfy your curiosity?'

'Hardly. Are all the men in England blind? Wasn't there someone else who could have escorted you? What about the latest man in your life?' he probed, ignoring the way her eyes flashed angrily at the cross-questioning.

She squared up to him. 'What exactly do you want to know, Pierce, the state of my love life?' she charged, hot colour storming into her cheeks at his audacity.

'Judging by the state of tension you're in, I'd say you haven't got one. Either that, or his technique is so bad he leaves you frustrated,' he returned, taking her breath away, so that she stared up at him rather like a stranded fish.

'How dare you?'

'Does that mean I'm wrong or I'm right?' he enquired sardonically.

'That means you've one hell of a nerve, and I've no intention of answering such a personal question,' she rejoined angrily, and he laughed.

'I think you just did. However, if men haven't taken up your time, what have you been doing these past five years?'

'Getting on marvellously well without you, I'm happy to say.'

'So I see,' he agreed, pricing her clothes and jewels with little difficulty. 'You've been living high off the hog. Who paid for it all—Daddy?' he jeered, and she saw red again.

'Wrong. I earned the money to pay for my clothes by sheer hard work. My jewellery was a twenty-first birthday present, and I don't think even you would begrudge me that!' Alix countered hotly.

'Spoken like a lioness defending her cub,' he drawled ironically, and Alix decided she had had just about enough.

'Why not? You might enjoy hitting people when they're down and can't defend themselves, but I don't. In fact, I don't even like associating with people like that, so if you don't mind...' She sent him a chilly smile, and would have brushed past him, only his hand shot out to grasp her wrist and halt her departure.

'Not so fast. We still have to talk,' he said shortly.

She attempted to shake him off, but he resisted effortlessly. All she could do was fix him with an unwavering glare. 'As far as I'm concerned, we've said more than enough,' she retorted frigidly.

Pierce shook his head. 'Darling, we haven't even begun to talk. But you're right, this isn't the time or place. I'll be at your office at ten o'clock tomorrow morning.'

How dared he think he could just waltz back into her life and take it over? 'You may be there, but I won't see you. I have appointments all day, and into the foreseeable future,' she informed him with great satisfaction.

He released her wrist, but only to bring his hand up to catch her chin, forcing their gazes to lock. 'Make room, or the only appointment you'll have is with the official receiver! And if that isn't warning enough, stop thinking about yourself and start thinking of your employees instead. This may be your last chance of saving their jobs. It's on your head, Alix. Can you afford your pride?' His eyes bored into hers for a second longer, then he set her free. 'Until tomorrow,' he promised, and it was he who left, with a brief nod.

Boiling with impotent anger, she watched his tall, broad-shouldered figure walk away. How she longed to tell him to go to hell, but his words stopped her—as he must surely have known they would. He also knew that she would see him tomorrow, for the sake of the very jobs she had been trying so hard to save, but with no success. It had been a bitter pill to swallow, the sense of failure. Now here was Pierce, implying he might be ready to do something, and, hate him though she might, she knew she couldn't afford to turn him away.

The knowledge left a bitter taste in her mouth for the rest of the evening. She left early, but didn't go straight home. Instead she took a taxi to the London hospital where Stephen Petrakos still lay in Intensive Care. Three weeks ago he had suffered a massive heart attack, and had had at least one smaller one since. It was a miracle he had survived at all, and it was while his life hung in the balance that she had discovered the perilous state of affairs his publishing empire was in. While the doctors were slowly winning the battle for her father's life, she was still trying to save his company.

Her mother looked up from her knitting as Alix walked into the room, a tiny, fragile woman whose wan face creased into a welcoming smile on seeing her daughter. 'Hello, darling, did you have a nice time?'

Alix bent to kiss a smooth cheek. Emily Petrakos was the kind of woman whose sweet nature inspired protectiveness in those around her, never more so than in her family. It had become second nature to shield her mother from the harsher side of life long before her father's illness, the cause of that being the mess she was striving helplessly to sort out now. But even though her mother must surely suspect something was wrong, if her father had said nothing to his wife, then she could say nothing either. Which was why Alix now fixed a cheerful smile on her face.

'Oh, you know how those things are. The cause was good, and that was what mattered. How's Dad?'

'Sleeping now, but he was terribly restless earlier. I do wish he'd tell us what's wrong,' her mother sighed, biting her lip in concern, and unwittingly confirming her daughter's suspicions.

Alix gave her a hug. 'Try not to worry, Mum. You know how Dad hates to be ill, especially when it takes him away from the business. However, I'm in control of things temporarily, and I think I may have some good news for him soon.' Mentally she crossed her fingers, in the desperate hope that it would be true.

'You're such a comfort, Alix. Heaven knows where I'd be without you,' Emily Petrakos declared, only to have her smile replaced by a frown. 'But you look tired, dear. Aren't you sleeping?'

Sleep was a scarce commodity these days, and even when she found some her dreams were troubled. None of which she was about to admit to. 'I'm fine, really, it's just been a long day today. I intend to go straight to bed when I get home. Don't forget to get some sleep yourself, Mum. You know it will only upset Dad more if he sees you looking worried.'

'You make me sound like a tonic!'

Alix laughed softly. 'You are, and the best one he could have.' Stifling a yawn, she glanced at her watch. 'I'd better go. I'll pop in again tomorrow. Give Dad a kiss for me, and tell him to stop worrying,' she urged, before kissing her mother once more and leaving.

Her flat was near the river in Chelsea. It was small, but suited her perfectly. She had rented it before her short-lived marriage, and, because she had refused to accept any financial benefit from her divorce, had been glad to return to it and nurse her wounds. She let herself in with a sigh of relief, only feeling safe when the bolts had been shot. It was Pierce who made her feel that way—as if she should run, and keep on running. Walking through to the lounge, she dropped her coat on the couch and went to pour herself a brandy. She needed it. His presence had been a shock. She had never expected to see him again after the divorce. After all, she thought, lips twisting, why would he come back when he had already got everything he wanted?

Once she had believed she was the embodiment of the sentiment in those three words, but she had only been his tool. He had made his plans like a general. All the soft words and loving looks, right down to the vows they had exchanged, everything had been designed with one purpose—to get him within sight of his goal.

She hadn't known anybody could pretend like that. She had loved him, and she had believed he loved her. Her mouth twisted. But that was what she had been supposed to think. Her naïveté was like a scourge to her already lacerated soul. She had been a young twenty-one to his vastly more experienced twenty-nine. He couldn't have known for certain that she would fall in love with him, only that he knew enough about women to be able to make it a distinct possibility.

Shivering, Alix curled up in an armchair. Pierce had been right about her love life. She didn't have one, and was there really any wonder? What she had suffered at his hands had made her fear the fire like any sane person. Never again would she trust any man with her happiness. Oh, she had men who were friends, and whom she sometimes dated, but although she knew some of them would like to deepen the relationship she had always been careful to keep them at a distance.

Her friends had stopped asking her why she had changed so after her return from America when she had stonewalled every question. Though they still tried to pair her up, it was half-hearted at best, and they obeyed her unspoken wish for privacy.

She closed her eyes. Stopping questions was one thing, stopping memories was something else. In the beginning they had been her scourge to remind her of what must never happen again. The scenes had been played over one by one, but although they had haunted her, waking and sleeping, for the past five years, the intervals between had lengthened. She hadn't thought of him for a long time, but tonight everything returned with a vengeance.

Pierce had been so clever, manipulating her into believing what she wanted to believe—that he loved her. Only he hadn't. That had been made manifestly obvious to her in one short hour. He had acted out his part with such consummate skill that it wasn't till the morning after the wedding that she discovered the man she had married was nothing but a sham.

On the day that should have been the beginning of their life together she had finally met the real Pierce Martineau...

CHAPTER TWO

IT HAD been a hard day at work. Not that Alix minded hard work at all. She was coming to the end of a six-month exchange, and finding out how a sister company worked would surely put her in good stead for her return to England, now only a few weeks away, where she would take up her job as a junior executive in the publishing business her father had built up. However, her new friends socialised at night with just the same energy as they used during the working day, and she wasn't quite used to partying to all hours. Which was why she was feeling tired, and why she was thankful that tonight she had already arranged a visit to the theatre with some friends of her father's.

The play was excellent, and she was discussing it enthusiastically in the foyer during the first break when she felt eyes on her. It was an uncanny sensation, raising the hairs on her flesh, and it was almost as if those unknown eyes were compelling her to turn around. Which she did because she couldn't help herself, eyes scanning the crowd for mere seconds before they locked with eyes of such a vivid blue, they seemed to spear her to her soul. Her lips parted on a silent gasp as she seemed unable to tear her gaze away from the man who stood mere yards away. In those seconds something elemental flew between them, then someone claimed his attention, and she was released.

Instantly Alix turned away, but a stronger compulsion had her looking back over her shoulder. She was aware of her heart galloping madly and unconsciously pressed a hand to her throat. He was still talking, and she could only see his profile, but even that caused a jolt of awareness to lock her stomach muscles. He had to be the most handsome man she had ever seen. His suit fitted him like a glove, and as he was standing with his hands in his pockets the jacket was pushed back, and she had the perfect view of his long legs and muscular thighs. A wave of heat swept through her as her body responded in a way it never had before. Her blood seemed to sing and her mouth went dry. And as she raised stunned eyes she saw him excuse himself and begin to walk towards her.

For a second time she looked away, but the tension in her body alerted her to the exact moment he stopped beside her. Her brain had stopped functioning a long time ago, but she heard her companions greet him with pleasure. His reply was said in a deep, mellow voice that sent shivers up and down her spine. Then she heard her name, and had to pull herself together quickly.

'Alix, we'd like you to meet a good friend of ours, Pierce Martineau,' Robert Wells declared jovially. 'This little lady is English, and the daughter of an old friend, Alix Petrakos.'

Automatically Alix held out her hand, knowing she must be staring helplessly up at him like an idiot. 'How do you do?' she greeted huskily, and felt the hand which had swallowed hers tighten fractionally. It was like touching a live wire, and she knew from his indrawn breath that he felt it too.

Pierce Martineau returned that stare silently for a moment, and Alix had the strangest feeling that he was shocked. Then he smiled and cleared his throat. 'Forgive my rudeness, but I was quite bowled over by your accent. Add that to your beauty, and a mere male is helpless,' he excused himself with lethal charm.

'Careful, Alix, Pierce has quite a reputation!' Olivia Wells warned with a laugh. 'He's the original wolf.'

Pierce seemed to release Alix's hand reluctantly, his attention remaining on her even as he responded to the other woman. 'Stop maligning me, Livvy, or you'll scare her off.'

Delicate colour washed into Alix's cheeks, as she licked her lips nervously, an act which his eyes followed minutely, their colour deepening dramatically. 'I prefer to make my own judgements about people,' she declared daringly, and watched his lips curve as he smiled.

'I'm relieved to hear it,' he said softly, making Alix feel as if they were the only two people in the room. 'Petrakos? That sounds Greek, not English.'

'My family came from Greece after the war. My mother's English, and I was born there,' she replied rather breathlessly, just as the bell went for the second act. Biting her lip, she realised they had to go, but the prospect of never seeing this man again made her feel cold inside.

His hand on her arm detained her. 'May I take you to supper after the play?'

Her heart seemed to be lifted by wings of joy, and she was sure it must be mirrored on her face. Before it fell as she recalled she was the Wellses' guest. 'I'd like to, but we've already got a table booked.'

'It seats four,' Olivia observed wryly. 'Join us, Pierce.'

'It will be my pleasure,' he accepted, all the while keeping his eyes on Alix, who felt she could drown in their fathomless depths. 'Until later, then,' he promised huskily, and with a last smile walked away.

'Well!' Olivia declared wonderingly. 'I don't think I've ever seen Pierce react like that before. You've certainly made a hit there, Alix.'

She certainly hoped so. Though she had never really believed in it before, Alix knew she had fallen in love at first sight. The remainder of the play was lost on her, for her thoughts were miles away. Though she clapped at the end, she couldn't have said what occurred, and it was only when they finally emerged into the foyer and she saw Pierce waiting by the door that life seemed to flow back into her.

Supper at a nearby restaurant was raised above the ordinary by the new-found feelings which swelled her heart. Afterwards, there was never any doubting that Pierce would drive her home. He walked her right to the door of the apartment she was renting, taking the key from her and opening the door. Returning the key, he held on to her hand, frowning down into her upturned face.

'Alix Petrakos,' he murmured on a strange sighing moan. 'Who would have thought that you would come into my life and turn it upside-down?'

The statement did funny things to her heart. 'Have I?'

A wry smile quirked his lips. 'Oh, yes, most definitely. I never expected you.'

She didn't quite know what to make of that. 'I didn't expect you, either. I came here to work, not...' She floundered to a halt.

'Not,' Pierce agreed, looking deep into her eyes. 'Perhaps it isn't the done thing to kiss you on our first date, but God knows I want to!'

The passion in his voice stole her breath, and she shivered. 'Is this a date?'

'The first of many,' he promised throatily, drawing her towards him, but gently, so that she could refuse if she wanted to.

Alix didn't want to. She went into his arms, feeling as if she belonged there. His head dipped, and his lips brushed hers. Tentatively at first, almost as if he was afraid, his tongue-tip traced delicately over her lips. She gasped as the *frisson* of pleasure chased along her nerves, and her lips parted, allowing him the freedom to caress the sensitive inner skin. A tiny cry of delight escaped her throat, and with a groan he caught a hand in her hair, pulling her closer as he deepened the kiss with an erotic mastery. Alix, who had always thought kissing rather overrated, suddenly found her senses rioting at the pleasure they were receiving, and which they urged her to return. Arms clinging around his neck, at first tentatively, then more boldly, she welcomed the stroking thrust of his tongue with her own. By the time Pierce dragged himself away, they were both breathing fast.

Holding her at arm's length, he closed his eyes and breathed in deeply. 'No more. You would drive a saint to lose control, and, as Livvy told you, I'm no saint,' he growled, then, seeing the downward turn of her bruised lips, brushed his thumb over them.

'I don't want a saint,' she returned dangerously, and shivered at the way his eyes glittered. She'd never wanted anybody, until Pierce.

Taking her hand, he brushed it with his lips. 'At this point a wise man would withdraw, but it seems I cannot. Have dinner with me tomorrow.'

It never even entered her head to say no, but she had no idea just how much her 'yes' would change her life.

She went to dinner with him the following evening, and the hours flew by. By the time he drove her home, she was fathoms-deep in love with him. He was so easy to talk to, interested in everything she said. When he talked about himself, she was so busy watching the play of expressions on his face, and listening to the silky sound of his voice, that she could hardly remember a word he had said, but she was captivated even so.

He was like no other man she had ever met. Handsome, exciting, endlessly intriguing, he swept her off her feet. Used to being pursued by men who either wanted to know her because of who she was, or who were only interested in adding her to their list of conquests, Pierce was like a breath of fresh air. Oh, she knew he wanted her, as the passion of his goodnight kisses made plain enough, yet at no time did he attempt to rush her into bed. Her response to him was just as potent, but made all the more electrifying for being held in check.

He chose to satisfy other senses. Every date became an adventure as he introduced her to new and exciting experiences. One day they might succumb to the lure of grand opera followed by a late supper at an exclusive restaurant, the next would find them walking barefoot on the beach, eating seafood on the pier. Yet all the time that underlying attraction was there. He made exciting love to her, but was always in control. Then one evening, when the frustration which had her tossing restlessly in her bed at night made her protest at his withdrawal, he drew her up beside him on her couch and brought her gaze up to his with a hand beneath her chin.

'When I take you to bed, Alix, it will be to consummate a marriage, not an affair,' he declared huskily.

As she gazed up at him, lips still throbbing from his passionate kisses, tears sprang to her eyes. 'You want to marry me?' she gasped incredulously, because although it was what she wanted she hadn't been sure that Pierce wanted anything more than an affair.

He smiled wryly. 'I rather think I ought to, before my control runs out.'

Her eyes probed his, wanting to be sure. 'You know you don't have to marry me, Pierce,' she offered, because it was true. She loved him too much to deny him anything.

His blue gaze scalded her. 'I know, but it's marriage or nothing. Or are you saying you don't want to marry me?' he accused, and she shook her head swiftly.

'Oh, no! I do want to marry you, Pierce. I love you desperately,' she cried, flinging her arms up around his neck and burying her face in his shoulder.

After a second, his own arms closed about her. 'Then we'll be married as soon as I can arrange it,' he declared thickly. 'You don't mind if it's just the two of us? No friends, no family?'

So happy, she rubbed her cheek against his. 'Mum and Dad won't mind, just so long as I'm happy.'

So, without telling a soul, they were married in Los Angeles just a few days later, taking witnesses from off the street, and rushed straight from the wedding chapel to the airport to catch a flight to New York. It didn't worry her that she really knew very little about him, except that he was American and a businessman. They had fallen in love, and their time was too precious to worry about such mundane matters. She knew he was successful, but it wouldn't have mattered if he wasn't. Love, she discovered, was all they needed to make them happy.

It was quite late when they arrived at his apartment. Alix suddenly found she was nervous. This would be the first time they had really been alone together, and the promise of the night ahead made her shiver with equal measures of excitement and alarm. She had never made love with anyone in all her twenty-one years, while Pierce was undoubtedly experienced, and she didn't want to disappoint him. Especially when he appeared to be in such a strange mood. He had been quiet on the flight, preoccupied, and when he had spoken there had been an odd stiltedness in his manner which she found a little unnerving.

When it continued into the meal his housekeeper had left for them, but which neither of them was doing justice to, she felt forced to speak. 'Is everything all right?'

Without looking at her, Pierce continued cutting his meat, but then, with a muffled oath, he threw aside his knife and fork, meeting her startled gaze with a look she had come to know so well, and which set her heart thumping in her chest.

'No, it isn't. There's only one thing I'm hungry for, and that isn't food. I want you, Alix. I've waited as long as I can, but my patience has finally run out,' he declared gruffly, and rose to his feet.

She understood then the reason for his preoccupation, and didn't protest when he picked her up and carried her to their bedroom, nor at the fervour with which he proceeded to make love to her so gloriously.

He awakened her fledgeling sensuality with a sensitivity which allowed her to find her own pace, caressing away her clothes, and inviting her to do the same to him. Any fear she had had evaporated in the growing heat of passion, stoked by the caress of his hands on her silken skin, and the touch of his mouth on her breasts.

He aroused her slowly, taking infinite care, his mouth and hands teasing until she was moving restlessly beneath him, her hands reaching out to touch him. His receptivity, the moaning sighs he gave that revealed the pleasure her touch was giving him, invited her to be bolder, and all her inhibitions faded away. It was not enough, and she told him so with every pleading twist of her body. Only then did he begin to make love to her with an urgency that soon had them locked together, straining towards a goal she had never reached before. When he took her, the pain was fleeting, forgotten as Pierce showed her a world of dazzling pleasure, taking her way beyond herself in a kaleidoscopic explosion which had her crying out, and hearing his own cry echo in her wake.

Alix stirred in the large double bed, coming awake to the tingling knowledge that Pierce lay beside her. Her husband. A warm glow of pure happiness spread through her system at the sound of that. No longer was she plain Alix Petrakos, but Mrs Pierce Martineau.

Turning her head on the pillow, her lips curved as she studied the back of his head, his dark hair rumpled by more than mere sleep. The memory started an altogether different glow inside her. Their union had been perfect. Everything she had ever hoped and more. She had fallen asleep in his arms, blissfully content. But that had been last night. It was morning now, and all she had to do was reach out and touch him, and Pierce would respond. Her heart gave a skip and settled into a faster rhythm, the fine hairs on her body rising as her nerve-ends came to prickling life. Smiling, she rolled over beneath the silk sheet, reaching out one slim hand to slide about his waist.

It was a move she never completed, because at her first touch the man beside her jack-knifed away, sitting up, thrusting back the cover.

'Don't touch me!' The rasping tones, so harshly alien, shocked her into immobility—but only for a millisecond; then she too sat up, watching in total incredulity as the supple, naked figure of her husband moved away from the bed with a stiff-legged stride. One visibly trembling hand pushed the tumble of long platinum locks from her eyes. Large grey eyes, rimmed by dusky lashes, were suddenly clouded with disbelief and hurt.

'What?' She breathed the question on a note that hovered uncertainly between hopeful humour and pending horror.

The tall, slim-hipped, dark-haired figure of her husband seemed actually to stiffen at the sound of her voice, but he didn't halt his progress to the *en-suite* bathroom. Gathering scattered wits, Alix was out of the bed in seconds, the sheet she used to cover her nakedness billowing about her legs as she followed him to the open door. He had to explain that remark if he wanted her to treat it as the joke it just had to be.

'Pierce!' Alix managed to keep her voice light by a monumental effort, but even so her underlying shock was plain. 'That wasn't funny, darling.'

Leaning casually against the sink, Pierce waited for the bowl to fill, turning off the water before swinging his head towards her. She wasn't able to hold back her gasp as his beautiful blue eyes surveyed her from her head to her toes with blood-chilling disdain. She felt as if he stripped her. Not of clothes, but of her dignity. She suffered a searing wave of humiliation never experienced before, and her eyes widened, something as cold and heavy as lead filling her stomach.

When Pierce spoke, there was insolence in his voice too. 'I never for a minute imagined it was.'

'Pierce!' She couldn't believe he would say something to hurt her so. Not this cold-bloodedly. It wasn't a joke. It was something more horribly real than that, and she had to find out just what it was before her world fell apart in tatters. 'What's happened? What's wrong?'

Pierce was busy applying shaving-foam, but he paused to spare her a mocking glance that seemed to diminish her. 'Whatever makes you think something is wrong?'

She floundered in a morass of confusion. Up until yesterday he had been so loving, and now... She cast about desperately in her mind for some sort of an answer, anything that would hold back the black tide of pain. 'Is it something I've done? Are you regretting marrying me?' It was the only thing she could think of.

He laughed at that, but without a single mitigating trace of humour. 'No, I had every intention of marrying you. It was what I wanted.'

It should have been the answer she wanted to hear, but there was an edge to it which struck a chill through her heart. He sounded so cold, so... unemotional. Like a wanderer in a maze, she knew there was only one road out of this hell, and that was to follow the trail he laid for her. 'You may have wanted it, but I know something's wrong. I'm not that much of a fool, however much I may seem to be to you now. I only know that, whatever it is, it's something we can solve together. That's what it's all about when two people love each other.' Her voice, for all her attempts at sounding reasonable, carried a note of desperation.

Her husband didn't even bother to pause in his shaving. 'Who said anything about loving each other?'

The offhand question was a mortal blow which set her rocking. Alix found that her voice had to be dragged from a painfully tight throat. 'But I love you, Pierce.'

'That much we do agree on.' He looked at her then, steely blue eyes daring her to follow up what he said.

She had no defence against the truth he wanted her to acknowledge. 'No!' Her cry was a hoarse denial, as a destructive pain tore through her.

Pierce calmly washed away the remaining soap and reached for a towel. 'No. Quite correct. A good night's sleep seems to have done wonders for your perception.'

Alix felt so weak that she had to hold on to the doorpost to stop from falling, while her other hand pressed tightly against her heart. 'You told me you loved me,' she whispered brokenly.

'If you think back clearly, you'll realise I never did use those actual words.'

Her tortured mind winged back to every conversation they had had, and knew it was true. The day she had told him she loved him Pierce had replied... Her eyes shot to his in anguish. She had thought he *had* told her, but his actual words had been that she couldn't know the depth of feeling he had in his heart for her! Not love! Never love, only...

Though it killed her, she had to know. 'Why did you marry me, Pierce?'

'Why? At the risk of sounding melodramatic, I married you for vengeance.'

The word bombarded her. 'Vengeance? But that makes no sense. For what? What have I done?'

She saw anger in his eyes then, a fury so great that it wiped out the terrible disdain. 'Can the granddaughter of Yannis Petrakos really not know? I can't believe that, my dear Alix. Search your memory, and I'm sure you'll find the truth. Of course, if you don't manage it, you can always come and ask me.' He controlled his anger with that mocking contempt. 'Now, if I'm going to get to the office for eight-thirty, I'd like to shower. For which I would prefer a little more privacy, if you don't mind. Or can it be that watching a man walk about naked is one of your more interesting peccadilloes?' Having sent that parting shot and watched it strike home, Pierce shut the bathroom door in her face.

Alix stumbled the few feet which separated her from the bed, and collapsed down on it. Her limbs were shaking with a palsy, her thoughts chaotic. The only fact which penetrated was that he didn't love her. The words went over and over in her mind like a record stuck in a groove. Which was why she was still sitting there when Pierce emerged from the bathroom minutes later and, after affording her one brief glance, proceeded to dress. White-faced, she watched him, the scales falling from her eyes. Everything about him was hard now; there was none of the loving softness left. He had sloughed that off with yesterday's travel-soiled clothes, and now he stood revealed to her in his true colours.

Having ignored her presence, once dressed in a dark grey business suit Pierce paused briefly before departing. 'My housekeeper's name is Mrs Ransome. Should there be anything you require you need only ask her.'

Alix didn't have the necessary composure to reply and Pierce didn't wait for one. Without another word he left her. Left her alone with her misery of betrayal and only her agonised thoughts for company. When, only minutes later, Mrs Ransome appeared to enquire if she required breakfast, Alix still hadn't moved. Her chalk-white face showed no sign of tears because none had fallen, but she wasn't numb either. She only wished she were, so that the pain would end.

Calmly she refused the food, going through the painful mechanics of smiling. 'No, thank you, Mrs Ransome. I'm still feeling rather jet-lagged.' That twentieth-century phenomenon would have been far easier to deal with than the truth, and a bubble of hysteria threatened to destroy what composure she had. She swallowed it back hastily. 'I think I need to rest more than eat.'

The housekeeper nodded wisely. 'Very good, Mrs Martineau. And may I take this opportunity of wishing you and Mr Pierce happy?'

Alix didn't know whether to laugh or cry. Happy? Yet she must have made some acceptable reply, because the housekeeper smiled and went out. The mask cracked then, as she lowered her head, the graceful arch of her neck revealing her terrible vulnerability. She didn't know what Pierce meant. Her family hadn't done anything to him. She had never heard his name mentioned. But Pierce had been so sure. He wanted vengeance, he said, and had set out on a course to deceive and entrap her just for that purpose. He had spent weeks pursuing her, wooing her, using every facet of charm that lay at his fingertips to persuade her of his affections—to claim her as his wife so that he could callously renounce it all this way.

Her hands came up to cover her face. But she had loved him so! How could he betray her like this? It wasn't human. It was unfeeling and . . . Lord help her, her heart felt as if it was being torn asunder, the pain of it ripping open nerves until they were raw and bleeding. Yet even as the pain grew it gradually gave birth to a cauterising anger.

She had done nothing to deserve this! It was a cry from the very depths of her heart, and her blood answered. Suddenly she wanted to hurt him as he was hurting her. The thought of it filled her stomach with a red-hot flame. The memory of how she had given all her love and trust to this man branded her soul. Hot tears burned her eyes, but she refused to shed them. He had brought her low, but he would never see her cry.

Alix came out of the past with a shiver. The brandy remained untouched in the glass, and she set it aside, rubbing some warmth into her arms with her hands. The revenge she had sought in her rage and pain had never materialised, because that had been only the beginning. Yet nothing that happened later had touched her the way that first betrayal had. The hurt had gone so deep that all else had compounded it, but could not make it worse.

Yet, as she had told Pierce, their brief marriage had taught her a lesson. A valuable one. Never again would she fall for a man's lies, nor give him any control over her life, so that he had the power to manipulate and hurt her. Nor would she ever allow her own emotions to lead her into those same dangerous waters, blinding her to everything.

She had had a warning tonight that his attraction was as potent as ever, and she deplored her own feminine weakness which made her vulnerable to him. She had to be on her guard. Whatever Pierce was here for, she had to keep a clear head and not let her emotions sway her judgement. It was the only way to stay one step ahead of him. She didn't trust him, had learned not to in the hardest way.

Whatever plan he had she would be wary of. She knew all about the Martineau company now. It was so diversified, it was doubtful if he'd ever be threatened with a take-over, hostile or otherwise. Whereas he had a habit of acquiring failing companies, splitting them into their constituent parts, and selling them off at a profit. If that was what he had in mind for Petrakos Publishing, then he could think again.

Yet Pierce's personal reputation was spotless. He had the proverbial Midas touch. There was scarcely a word written but to praise him. However, the businessman was one thing, the man another, as she knew to her cost. If the Petrakos empire weren't in such dire straits, she would have absolutely nothing to do with him. But she must force herself to swallow her pride and be practical for the sake of the thousands of livelihoods involved.

If she kept her mind on that, then she knew she could handle Pierce. She had grown up a lot in the last five years, and knew she was stronger mentally. She wasn't going to be a coward and run away. This time she was going to face up to him, and she was going to win.

It was a thought which put a tight smile on her lips as she finally made her way to her bedroom. Perhaps she would get her revenge after all.

CHAPTER THREE

THE following morning, Alix dressed with more than her usual care. This meeting with Pierce was going to be a battle of wills, and it would be in her own best interests to project a confident image. Which was why she chose an extremely businesslike black suit, enlivening it by pinning the diamond brooch she had inherited from her grandmother on the lapel, completing the ensemble by adding diamond studs in her ears and a simple gold rope at her throat.

Stepping in front of the mirror, she took stock of the view he would receive. Her make-up had been applied with polished efficiency which made it seem almost non-existent, and altogether she knew she looked good. A businesswoman, in complete control of her life. It was an image she had worked hard to build, earning the respect she now received, and she wasn't going to give it up without a fight.

The drive to the office was as stressful as ever, but today she was aware of an added edge. The very last thing Alix wanted was to arrive late, because she knew how hard it was to make up lost time. Keeping Pierce waiting wasn't part of her plan. She wanted him to see that she could be cool and efficient under pressure. Fortunately, the gods seemed to be on her side, and she was soon taking the lift from the underground car park where she left her car, rising swiftly to her office on the top floor.

Her secretary was already hard at work, and Alix halted by her desk. 'Good morning, Ruth.'

The middle-aged woman looked up with a smile. 'Good morning, Alix. How's your father?'

'Improving, thankfully. Listen, you'd better leave the post for now. I've someone coming at ten o'clock, so I need you to clear the morning for me,' Alix responded, pink-tinted nails tapping out a tattoo on the polished surface of the desk.

Ruth reached for her diary. 'There was only Mr Johnson from the union pencilled in before lunch.'

Alix pulled a face. The union had been a headache for days now, and she had been fobbing them off until she had some definite news. 'Well, he won't like it, but it can't be helped. Try and squeeze him in this afternoon, but if not, tell him . . . tell him we've rescheduled because there might be light at the end of the tunnel.'

Ruth, as anxious about her job as anyone else, pricked up her ears. 'And is there?'

Alix chewed at her lips. 'That all depends on this meeting with Pierce Martineau,' she declared shortly.

'Are we talking the same Martineau as in the shipping line?' her secretary queried, visibly brightening.

Unfortunately the reference was not a welcome one to Alix. 'We are.'

Ruth was almost jigging in her seat. 'You know, for the first time I really do believe we might turn about. After all, he did wonders for that fleet, didn't he, turning a loss into a profit quicker than you could say it?'

'Yes, well, that's as maybe, but I'd rather you didn't spread any rumours until we know just what the deal is. Pierce Martineau never does anything for nothing,' Alix muttered broodingly.

'You sound as if you know him,' Ruth put in curiously, and Alix swiftly pulled herself together.

'Our paths have crossed before,' was all she cared to admit. 'I'll be in my father's office if you need me.'

Walking into her own office, she deposited her briefcase on the desk before letting herself into her father's spacious room via the connecting door. It seemed lifeless without his vital presence in the driving seat. Somehow she just couldn't imagine him not coming back here. Yet, if the doctors were right, then Stephen Petrakos would have to undergo a rapid change in lifestyle if he wanted to live much longer.

Crossing to the desk, she ran her hands over the soft leather of the chair, then slowly sank into its cushioned depth. She had the distinct impression of being swallowed up. It was too big for her. It needed another Stephen Petrakos to fill it. The realisation made her feel tired. She had stepped into her father's shoes because everyone had expected it of her, including herself. Now they expected miracles, and all she had done was singularly fail to put together a rescue package these last few weeks.

She swivelled round until she could see out of the window. She knew she was good at what she did, but that was on the publishing side of the business. Management was something outside her scope. She had done her best, but she doubted if anyone else knew the full extent of their financial problem. It was hard to believe the debts her father had mounted up. It had shown to her a man with a cavalier streak that she hadn't known existed. Although, from the meetings she had had with other managers, not everybody had been as blinkered as she. The company was drastically over-extended, and the size of the interest payments to be made on hefty bank loans arranged to start up new projects had made her feel sick. Money seemed to be flooding out, not in, and it was a nightmare. No wonder her father had had a heart attack. What the company needed was a large injection of cash and a firm hand at the wheel.

She groaned out loud. It was a bitter irony that the only person who possessed both of her requirements was her ex-husband. She didn't want to do business with him, because she knew in her bones that the price would be high. Last time it had been her grandfather who had suffered. It might not have been worth much, but the Petrakos shipping line had been his pride. Losing it had killed him, not directly, but in the long run.

Though her gaze still remained on the world outside, it was another scene she was visualising on the projection screen of her mind. The Petrakos shipping line. Five years ago she hadn't even known of its existence, but it was something she could never forget—as she would never forget that day when she had first heard it from the lips of Pierce Martineau...

The sound of the apartment door opening and closing, followed by the muffled but recognisable tones of her husband, brought Alix's head up from her knees. She turned startled eyes on the clock, amazed to see that it was after seven in the evening. The time had passed her by as she sat curled up in a chair by the window, locked in a limbo where her senses were blessedly numb. She had been waiting for Pierce to come home. She hadn't left, as her pride had told her to, because she knew she had to face him one more time. He had killed her love for him. He had used her without thought for her feelings, and she needed to know why. If she deserved nothing else, she at least deserved to be told the truth, however painful it might be.

Alix rose stiffly to her feet. Her body felt as if it was one big ache, and although earlier she had put on jeans and a Guernsey sweater she still felt cold. She knew it was reaction; she only hoped that nothing showed when she saw Pierce. He knew he had hurt her, for he had deliberately set out to do so, but she'd be damned if she'd let him see just how much. Facing him again now wouldn't be easy. Perhaps it was the hardest thing she had ever done. Only anger could give her the strength she needed.

The apartment was large, and all she knew of its layout was the dining-room and the bedroom. She had looked forward to exploring, but somehow this morning she just hadn't felt like it! The wry humour lodged in her throat and, standing in the hallway, she quickly looked around. To her left a door stood ajar and light spilled from it. If Pierce was anywhere, then she might as well start her search there.

Alix found herself in a spacious modern lounge. Velvet curtains covered most of one wall, which meant it was probably all window. Elegant couches and armchairs made seating areas around low coffee-tables, the carpet muffled even the heaviest footstep, and the paintings on the walls were originals. At any other time she would have found it a charming room, but she was far too tense for anything so facile. There was a fireplace opposite, and although nothing burned there she crossed to it, soft-footed, as if by association her icy fingers would warm.

The chink of ice on glass brought her head shooting round. Pierce was standing by a drinks trolley watching her through hooded eyes.

'Would you like a drink before dinner?'

The matter-of-fact question was like a slap in the face. How could he be so calm after what had happened this morning? It was almost as if *nothing* had happened! Her anger grew. 'No, thank you,' she ground out through her teeth, watching him walk towards her with the economical stride which was part of his animal magnetism, and which had once made her shiver in anticipation.

There was a mocking twist to his lips as he came into the circle of light thrown out by the lamp on the sofa table. 'You've gone into mourning, I see.'

Alix glanced down at her clothes, realising for the first time that they were black. It hadn't been intentional, merely the first things that came to hand. Yet it was bitingly apt. She worked at her throat, saying thickly, 'Something died today, Pierce, and I still don't know why.'

Pierce came closer, resting one arm along the mantelpiece. 'Mrs Ransome tells me you spent the day in our bedroom.'

Alix found his closeness almost intolerable, yet she forced herself to make no move away from him, lest he believe he had her on the run. 'I'm asking you to tell me why you've done this. What you meant about my grandfather.'

For a moment he merely stared down at her, as if gauging whether her ignorance was real or not. Then he shrugged carelessly. 'You and I have Greek blood in our veins, my dear Alix. An oath is not to be taken lightly, and I'm keeping a promise I made,' he enlightened her smoothly. 'As for where Yannis Petrakos comes into the picture, I'll be only too happy to tell you, in my own good time.'

His arrogance sickened her, and the only way to keep her hands from his handsome face was to ball them into fists at her sides. 'I want to know now,' she insisted angrily.

Blue eyes ran over her stiff figure with lazy insolence. 'After dinner.'

How easily he made her feel like the pawn he thought her to be. 'Oh, God, I hate you!' The words were almost a sob, and she pressed her lips together tightly so as not to let another escape.

However, she could have screamed and he would only have looked amused, just as he did now. 'Do you? Only yesterday you loved me.'

Gasping at that studied cruelty, she stared into his eyes and murder was in her heart. 'Why didn't you challenge me when we met if this oath of yours was so important?'

'Haven't you worked that out for yourself? You've had all day. Because I needed you to be my wife. Without that, you could have walked away scot-free.'

Her heart felt as if it was being squeezed in a vice. He was shredding her, leaving her with nothing. Nothing except a fierce pride, which lifted her chin a fraction. 'I can still do that now. Or are you saying I'm your prisoner?'

A small chilling smile curved his lips. 'You can go any time you want to. I don't need you as a hostage,' he confirmed easily. 'All I needed was you as my wife. And you are that, aren't you, Alix? In name and in the flesh.'

Alix felt what little colour she had drain away. 'Are you telling me you slept with me just to consummate the marriage?'

One eyebrow lifted disdainfully. 'Could you be foolish enough to imagine I'd leave any loopholes? Fulfilling the oath depended on it.'

Nearly choking on an upsurge of nausea, she shook her head in appalled disbelief. 'How could I have been foolish enough to think I loved you?'

Lids lowered over blue eyes as Pierce reached out to run the knuckles of his hand down her cheek. 'Can you be so sure that you don't now?'

There was something in his touch that seemed to tug at her heart, and, hating herself for it, Alix curled her lip in contempt. 'There's no love left for you, only hate.'

His lips parted on a short bark of mocking laughter. 'Maybe not love, but what about desire? Shall we put *that* to the test?'

His callousness took her breath away. He had just told her he had made love to her because he had to, not because he wanted to, and now he wanted to prove that she was still his any time he wanted her. 'Don't you dare touch me!'

Suddenly there was the strangest look in his eyes. 'Never dare me, Alix, that's the worst thing you could do,' he declared huskily, and caught her as she turned to flee, pulling her back, struggling, against his chest, pinning her arms with his and forcing her head still with a hand clamped in her hair. There was a moment when their eyes locked, hers spitting loathing and his carrying that odd expression she couldn't interpret, then his head dropped and Alix prepared herself for the assault.

Only it didn't turn out like that. His lips were gentle and warm, dropping kisses now here, now there, until she couldn't bear it. Her heart was wrenched apart as she suffered an embrace that seemed to encompass a world of loving, and yet was a mockery of the very word. Sobbing, she tried to pull away, but all he did was deepen the kiss, using tongue and lips to seduce her. He knew her so well. He knew the precise moment when she would stop fighting and start kissing him back, and there was nothing she could do about it.

Her response stripped her bare, and when Pierce released her at last her eyes loomed huge in her ashen face. His own were glittering so brightly that they dazzled.

'It's not that easy, is it?'

If he wanted to make her feel cheap, then he couldn't have chosen a better way. 'I never thought I could despise any human being as much as I do you. What have you proved? That you can still turn me on? Maybe you can, and maybe it would amuse you to have me in your bed again. But you'd take me knowing that I'd hate every touch of your hands. My response has nothing to do with how I feel, and I feel only hatred for someone who could do what you have done to me today!' Her voice was thick with that hate, and a bitter self-loathing that she could not, even now, resist him. She turned away abruptly, but only got two steps on shaky legs before his voice halted her.

'Where are you going?'

She shot him a look full of revulsion. 'Back to my room until you're ready to talk to me.' She couldn't bear to be near him.

The tension emanating from him was awesome, and his voice correspondingly terse. 'If you want to know the facts, then you'll join me for dinner. I insist,' he added the last as she made to protest.

Balked, Alix turned back, knowing that although she never wanted to see him again she had to know everything. Taking a seat on the couch furthest away from him, she forced herself to look him in the face. 'Very well, if it amuses you. I'll have that drink now.' She needed it quite badly.

'I wouldn't say it amuses me,' Pierce said shortly, as he went to pour her a drink, returning with her usual martini.

Alix avoided his eyes, taking the glass, using extreme care to make sure their fingers didn't touch. Silence fell, and she had no intention of attempting to make polite conversation. This was no longer a honeymoon, and she the blushing bride. This was attrition, and she would not pretend otherwise. So it was a relief when there came a tap on the door and Mrs Ransome announced dinner. However, the mere thought of food was nauseating, and Alix called upon all her reserves of composure to enable her to take her seat at the table. But having got that far she made no attempt to eat what was placed before her, nor even to pretend that she had. Pierce regarded her from across the table, unamused by her still, silent figure.

'This is really very good, you should try it,' he encouraged after a moment, indicating the soup.

Her eyes battled with his. 'Is that an order?' she asked insolently, and his jaw tensed.

'Do you intend to starve yourself?'

'Because of you? Never!'

He smiled grimly at that. 'Then have some soup, Alix. According to Mrs Ransome you've eaten nothing all day.' There was steel in Pierce's voice, mixed up with, of all things, an impatient concern. 'Must I come round there and make you?'

Alix resorted to sarcasm. 'What's the matter? Afraid it wouldn't reflect well on you if I faded away?'

Sitting back in his chair, Pierce eyed her grimly. 'I'm afraid of nothing. I'm merely doing what has to be done. It has never been my intention to make you ill.'

Her jaw became set. 'Then you'd better either get out of my sight or let me go, because just seeing you sickens me!' she snapped back, not caring if it sounded childish or not.

He smiled but it failed to reach his eyes. 'Don't worry, I've no wish to prolong our acquaintance. Once I have what I came for, you need never see me again.'

Alix could feel the muscles in her face tighten up at that. 'I wish I'd never seen you!' she cried, just as the housekeeper bustled back into the room. His reply had to wait until Mrs Ransome had removed the soup dishes and replaced them with the main course.

Alone again, Pierce shrugged powerful shoulders. 'We would always have met, Alix. Some things are meant to be.'

She almost laughed. Now he wanted her to believe that the gods had something to do with it! 'I don't believe in such superstitious mumbo-jumbo. You planned everything down to the smallest detail, leaving nothing to chance. Such arrogance! Tell me, what would you have done if I had been engaged to be married?'

'I would have done my best to break it up, of course.'

She believed him. A man who had done what Pierce had would not have balked at an existing engagement. Because whatever it was he thought her family had done, it was serious enough for any action, however underhand. 'I believe you would, and I have nothing but contempt for you.'

Her emotional outburst just seemed to bounce off him. 'Having got that off your chest, and as neither of us seems to be enjoying the meal, we may as well go along to the study.'

Her heart lurched, but she stood up quickly, following him out and down the passage to another closed door. Switching on the light, he urged her inside. It was a mellow room with shelves full of books, a well-used desk at one end, and a grouping of chairs surrounding another mock-fireplace. Next to it was a unit given over to cups and photographs. It was to this that Pierce's hand at her back was urging her. He reached up to one particular shelf, retrieved a framed photograph and handed it to her.

'Do you recognise anyone?'

She frowned, then quickly glanced down at the fading print. It was a dockyard scene, where two dark-suited men stood shoulder to shoulder, dwarfed by the ships behind them. At first she saw nothing, but then something in one of the men's stern faces made her take a closer look.

'It's my grandfather!' she exclaimed in surprise.

'And mine. George Andreas.'

'Andreas? But that's Greek, and your name is Martineau.'

'My grandparents were Greek, but they left Greece after the war and emigrated to America. Their daughter, my mother, married an American, Lawrence Martineau, and I was born here,' Pierce expanded, one long finger still pointing to the other man before moving on to the background. 'And these are the Andreas fleet.'

In her perplexity, she forgot to be angry. 'I don't understand. You're saying our grandfathers knew each other?'

He laughed shortly. 'I'm saying they were the best of enemies. To prove it, Yannis Petrakos stole the fleet from my grandfather.'

'Stole it?' Alix gasped, then thrust the photograph back to him. 'Don't be ridiculous! Grandfather doesn't own any ships!'

The smile that spread over Pierce's lips was grimly amused. 'I can assure you he does. A few ships lie rotting away in a North African dockyard, all that's left of the Petrakos shipping line. Proud ships which once bore the name of Andreas. Yannis Petrakos always wanted those ships. They were an élite fleet, and to own them would have meant wealth, prestige, acceptance into the upper echelons of society—three things he was hungry for. He sought to get them by marrying the owner's daughter, for they were to be part of her dowry, but she was already betrothed and would not look at him. That woman was my grandmother, and the ships came to my grandfather on their marriage. From that day on, Petrakos hated both of them, and swore to destroy my grandparents and the ships any way he could. What he could not have, none should have. After the war, he found the perfect way. He produced papers—forged, of course—which would prove my grandfather was a collaborator. Generously, he offered my grandfather a way out. If he signed over the ships, the papers would disappear. If not, the whole family would be shot.

'Of course it wasn't true, but there was no way of proving it, whereas Yannis Petrakos had links with the black market, and ways of getting what he wanted. So he finally got the ships, because my grandfather loved his family. He lost everything, but he took an oath that one day he would get his ships back. He came to America and started a new life, made a new fortune, but he never forgot. It broke his heart to see the way the fleet was slowly being allowed to sink into disrepair. Many times he offered to buy it, but Petrakos always refused. When he had no further use for them, he simply allowed the ships to rot away.

'When my grandfather died, he made me swear an oath that I would do what he had been unable to do. Petrakos has refused to sell to me, and so I see no reason to keep hitting my head against a brick wall. I looked around for another way, and found you. You are the key, Alix. I want the Petrakos shipping line, and you are going to get it for me!'

The strident buzz of the intercom startled Alix out of her painful memories once more, and she swivelled round to answer its summons.

'Yes, Ruth?'

'Mr Martineau is here, Miss Petrakos.'

Her heart knocked sickeningly, and she licked suddenly dry lips. 'Send him in, please, Ruth,' she directed, knowing that she should order coffee too, but her intention was that he shouldn't be there long enough to drink it.

She barely had time to smooth a hand over her hair and check that the buttons of her jacket were securely fastened before he walked into the room. She rose with studied politeness, very much aware of the atmosphere that entered the room with him. The very air about them seemed to crackle with it, and she found it unnerving, the way the office shrank, locking them into a kind of vacuum.

This morning he was the epitome of the successful businessman, his pale grey Italian suit sitting far too well on his tall frame, the white silk shirt and red tie setting off his dark hair, tanned skin and gleaming blue eyes. He was smiling with heavy irony as he crossed the floor to her.

'Good morning, Alix,' he greeted smoothly, holding out his hand, forcing her to grit her teeth and offer her own. It was swallowed up in his larger one, giving her the impression that she would be swallowed up too. As a consequence she pulled away far too abruptly, bringing a tinge of colour to her cheeks as his eyes danced.

'Mr Martineau,' she muttered coldly, pressing her fingers hard on the desk-top to stop their tendency to tremble. His touch had been like a live wire, shooting electricity up her arm. 'As you can see, I kept an appointment open for you; however, I would appreciate it if you didn't waste too much of my valuable time. I do have other people to see.'

Ignoring good manners, he seated himself opposite her, making himself comfortable. 'Sit down, Alix, and stop trying to impress me with your efficiency. We both know you're expecting nobody else. You've seen everybody who might have been expected to help already, with no success.'

Alix seethed inwardly. Did he have to rub her nose in it? It was one thing to know of her own failure, quite another to hear him speak of it. 'I never asked you to come,' she pointed out unnecessarily, sitting down only because her legs were so infuriatingly weak, that weakness brought about by an unwanted awareness of him. Nobody else had ever made her senses crackle the way he had, and still did, curse him.

'How is your father?' The disarming question made her frown.

'Do you really care? If not, I'd rather you didn't pay lip-service,' she retorted cuttingly, and Pierce's face grew stony.

'Whatever you've learnt in five years, good manners wasn't part of it. You're biting the hand that could feed you, Alix. You'd be better advised to remember that I'm under no obligation to help you. I can get up and leave at any time.'

The reproof was deserved, and she drew in a sharp breath, all the same hating having to kowtow to him. 'I'm sorry,' she managed to grit out, and he looked amused.

'Do I take it from that that you want me to stay?' he mocked.

Lord, he was a devil! Would he not be happy until he had seen her grovel? 'Yes.' The word was torn from a tight throat.

His lips curved. 'Then may I suggest you order some coffee? You're almost certain to need it.'

She didn't trust herself to answer, which he sensed and which only amused him more. She merely reached for the telephone and ordered the coffee. Sitting back, she took several deep breaths and forced herself to relax. She was letting him get to her, and that would always put her at a disadvantage. She had to let him see she was no longer a pushover.

'You implied last night that you might be able to help us,' she said in a far more ameliorating tone. 'What exactly did you have in mind?'

Pierce crossed his legs, eyeing the tip of one shining handmade shoe. 'As I understand it, the Petrakos

Publishing Group is heavily in debt. In order to save it, there needs to be not only a large injection of cash, but also a radical appraisal of the way the business is run. In short, having sorted out the debts, you need to cut back the business into a more manageable size. Correct?'

He certainly knew how to get to the bare bones of the problem, she thought, with acid respect. 'You know it is. However, you must know that I cannot agree to any sort of take-over without my father's consent.'

One eyebrow quirked. 'What makes you think I want to take over your business?'

She sent him an old-fashioned look. 'Don't take me for a fool. That's the way you work. Everyone knows it. You buy people out, cut the businesses up into little pieces and make a killing.'

Now both eyebrows described a mocking arc. 'Is that a criticism? Strange, I've never heard anyone else complaining. I deal fairly and squarely. People get the market value of their firms, and after that the risk is all mine. However, that isn't the sort of deal I'm offering you,' he told her quietly, and Alix found her nerves so tense, she couldn't possibly sit still.

She jumped to her feet. 'For goodness' sake, get to the point!'

'The point, my dear Alix, is that I am prepared to cover the debts. I am also prepared to inject sufficient cash to get the company rolling again,' Pierce announced silkily.

Alix stared at him as if he had gone mad. 'How? You've just said you aren't interested in taking the business over. Not even you are mad enough to just hand over money without some sort of return.'

Pierce steepled his fingers and regarded her over the top of them. 'You're absolutely right. I'm not. You see, what I'm offering is more in the nature of a gift than a loan, and I most certainly do expect to get a return.'

'A gift?' Struck dumb, Alix slowly sank back into her seat, wide grey eyes staring into his. She swallowed hard. It sounded too good to be true. 'What are your terms? I presume you have some?'

He inclined his head in acknowledgement. 'Most assuredly. The terms are these: I will hand over the required sums of money, and install a management team to review the company on the day that you, my dear Alix, become my wife.'

CHAPTER FOUR

'YOUR wife!'

For a moment Alix felt her senses swim, but then the blood rushed back with a vengeance, and she burst into sarcastic laughter, shaking her head in disbelief.

'You're insane! You have to be totally out of your mind!' she declared scathingly.

Not by a flicker did Pierce's expression change. 'That, of course, is a matter of opinion. It has absolutely no bearing on the matter in hand——'

'Except that you expect me to marry a madman!' she cut in savagely.

Now his expression assumed a studied blandness. 'I expect you to do the sensible thing. If I'm mad, as you say, then I'm still a very wealthy madman, and I'm offering you a way out of your difficulties. From all accounts, your only way out. The choice of accepting it is yours,' he informed her coolly.

Alix felt a nauseous anger churning in her stomach at the idea that he could have had the gall even to suggest such a thing. 'If you think, after the travesty of our first marriage, that I would ever, in any circumstances, contemplate marrying you again, then you aren't just mad, you're certifiable.' The burnt child dreads fire. It was a proverb she found no argument with.

'Stop being so melodramatic. You're a businesswoman, and this is a business deal,' Pierce commanded, with just the slightest edge to his voice.

Alix widened her eyes. 'You mean you'd be making the same offer if it were a man sitting here? How very accommodating of you!' she gibed.

Chilly blue eyes locked with hers. 'It wouldn't be wise to push me too far, Alix, My offer is a unique one, but can be withdrawn as easily as any other.'

She moved uncomfortably beneath that unwavering gaze. 'I'm surprised you haven't done so already. It would fit in with your *modus operandi*,' she couldn't help adding, even though she knew she was jeopardising her chances.

'I would have thought by now, things being the way they are, that you'd realise we do what we have to do. It is a trait common to each of us, for we both have Greek blood in our veins.'

Her eyes sent out spears of loathing in a vain attempt to slay him. 'Blood I would be only too happy to relieve you of. You see, I discovered five years ago that if there was one thing a Greek did well it was know how to hate. I took an oath too, Pierce, and that was to be revenged on you for what you did to me,' she told him passionately.

Amusement glittered in his eyes, but an emotion which seemed to be a cross between admiration and approval flickered across his face for a moment. 'I would have expected no less of a Petrakos.'

'And yet you would marry me? Would help my father? Do you really expect a Petrakos to take the word of an Andreas?'

'I expect you to take my word, along with my money, like any sensible person,' Pierce returned with a hint of anger of his own.

Alix let her eyes flash with scorn as she leant across the desk towards him. 'You make me sound a fool for looking a gift horse in the mouth, but you forget, I've heard of Troy too. I know only too well how much you should beware Greeks bearing gifts! So it really isn't any wonder I don't believe in your altruism. This is just some other scheme to get your filthy hands on another piece of the Petrakos inheritance!' she flung at him challengingly.

A muscle ticked in his jaw, the only visible sign that what she was saying had got through the steely thickness of his skin. 'There are only so many insults I am willing to take from you, Alix, so be advised. As to your claim about my intentions . . .' here he paused and gave a typically Greek shrug of the shoulders '. . . you are at liberty to believe what you like. I know that should I attempt to change your opinion it would only make you dig your heels in deeper. However, I will just say this. I only ever had one enemy, and that was Yannis Petrakos. The debt was paid when I got the shipping line.'

Alix could no longer sit still, and she rose agitatedly to her feet, pacing away, staring out of the window, yet seeing nothing. She didn't know if she really believed what she had just claimed or not. She was fighting as best she could, but without ammunition in her weapons, and with her back to the wall. His statement didn't help in any way, either. It only served to remind her of what she had never forgotten. Memory brought a renewed surge of pain, causing her fingers to curl into the frame. Defenceless or not, she had to go on.

'You used me then, and you want to use me now,' she stated hardily.

'On the contrary, I want to help you.'

Her laugh grated harshly on her own ears. 'Do you truly expect me to believe you'll be satisfied just to help me? Are you saying you'll let me go as soon as the money is paid over?' she taunted, disbelievingly.

Unseen, Pierce rose agilely to his feet, going to stand behind her, so that Alix had no trouble feeling the awesome tension in him. She tensed, too, yet not just at the latent power which he held in check. She was very much aware of his masculinity, of the spicy tang of his aftershave, and the heat which radiated off him.

'No,' he confirmed her doubts in a voice which ran with steel. 'The agreement is non-negotiable. You will remain my wife. There will be no divorce this time, and the marriage will be a very real one.'

Her breathing became restricted at the memories that conjured up, and her mouth twisted bitterly. Sex with Pierce had been more than just good, but then she had loved him. All that had changed. 'Will it give you some kind of warped satisfaction to take a woman who you know hates you?'

Pierce moved fractionally closer, so that she could feel the brush of his suit against her own, poignantly recalling the glide of flesh on flesh. She knew it was a deliberate move, and knew instinctively that her best defence was to stay quite still and ignore him.

'You may hate me, Alix, but I wonder if you've stopped wanting me?' he queried in an altogether different voice, one which sent shivers racing along her spine as his breath brushed her nape. 'You used to go up in flames in my arms.'

It was a goad she could not ignore despite her good intentions. She spun round, beside herself with anger, hand flashing out to slap his cheek so hard that it hurt her. 'Only an utter bastard would remind me of just how much of a fool I was! The answer is no, Pierce. A hundred times no. Now get out of here before I call Security and have you thrown out!' she ordered, hands thrust against his shoulders to push him away.

There was an answering anger in his blue eyes now. He moved swiftly, catching both her hands and forcing them round behind her back, hauling her resisting body hard up against his own. 'Oh, no! Not until I've proved one thing, you little hell-cat,' he bit out tautly, and brought his mouth down violently on hers.

It was a punishing assault which ground her lips against her teeth as she denied him entry, and had he continued with force she would have resisted him forever. But in seconds his attack changed, the pressure easing so that his lips barely brushed hers. Then the silken glide of his tongue stroked over the tender flesh, sending a *frisson* of pleasure along her nerves, relaxing muscles tensed to resist him. Taking swift advantage of that momentary softening, Pierce used one hand to hold both of hers and brought his free hand gliding up to cup her breast.

Alix felt the touch like a brand even through her jacket, and gasped as her breast swelled, the nipple pushing invitingly into his palm. With a grunt of satisfaction, he took her mouth, stroking her tongue erotically with his until she couldn't help but respond, tasting him as the fight went out of her and she collapsed against his chest. He released her hands then, lowering his to her hips and hauling her up close against him so that she could feel the hardness of his arousal. She groaned, hands coming round to clutch the cloth of his jacket as she floated away.

Oh, God, how she had missed this! Nobody else had ever made her feel as if she was burning up, ready to explode. Only Pierce... His name rent the sensual cocoon which he had been weaving around her, and reality returned with a sickening wave of self-disgust. She stiffened in his arms, and in an instant Pierce had released her, stepping away to gaze down mockingly into her agonised eyes.

'Would you still deny that you want me?' he demanded huskily, and she turned away, unable to bear the proof of her own response in the flush of passion lying warm on his cheeks, and the breathing which was as erratic as her own.

'I want you to go,' she said shortly, disgust at herself for being unable to resist him making the words more a request than an order.

'Not until we've settled this,' Pierce refused pointblank. His eyes narrowed thoughtfully on her averted face. 'You say you want revenge. What better way is there than to marry me?' he proposed levelly, once more fully in control of himself.

Swallowing the bitterness of knowing how helpless she was, Alix returned to her seat, fingers gripping the arms until her knuckles grew white. 'I won't put my head in that noose again,' she declared with all the firmness she could muster.

After a moment Pierce came to sit on the edge of the desk, hemming her in, even as his words were backing her further and further into a corner. 'All right, then look at it this way. Stop thinking of yourself. You say you want to help your father, and I'm offering you the only way. Just how much did you really mean it? What became of family loyalty, Alix? What happened to personal loyalties, to those you love and who love you?'

Alix gasped as a shaft of pain lanced through her. How dared he ask that? No sacrifice would be too great for them! And yet no sooner had that instinctive statement been drawn up than so too was another more painful truth. By her refusal she was denying her father the only chance he had left. She had tried every other avenue, and this was the only one remaining. Pierce had always had perfect timing! Her voice was choked when she spoke. 'You're a sadist.'

Reaching across, he put one hand under her chin and forced her to meet his eyes. 'I'm a realist. All you have to do is agree to marry me, and three days from now the money will be in the bank. Your father's worries will be over,' he expanded pragmatically.

While hers would be just beginning. 'No!' Her answer shot back at him as she pulled free. 'Besides, my father would never accept money from you!' she attempted to justify herself.

'Why not? My name should speak for itself,' he said without boasting, because it was a fact. World-wide his name was a virtual guarantee of good intent, despite her earlier remarks. Then, a moment later, Pierce's eyes narrowed consideringly. 'Or are you trying to tell me, in some roundabout way, that you told him about our marriage?'

How she would have loved to be able to say yes, and that her father thought he was a bastard too, but that would mean she had broken her word to her grandfather. It was a catch-22 situation, leaving her only with the truth. 'Nobody knows,' she admitted reluctantly. 'But if I told him who you are, then I doubt very much if he'd accept, whatever the consequences!' she added, not wanting him to win every round as easily as he had so far.

Pierce looked mildly amused. 'I know you'd like to think so, but your father is a realist too. Why don't you try asking him?'

Her eyes flashed with a helpless anger. 'Don't think I won't.' Once again he had her reacting almost childishly. What had happened to all her poise and self-control when she needed them so badly? Silly question. Pierce had happened, and that was explanation enough.

As she might have expected, he laughed outright. 'I put nothing past you, darling Alix. But just remember, you can still tell him nothing about our brief marriage. Nor would it be wise to get your hopes up too high. Somehow I don't think he'll be the champion you expect when it comes to an arranged marriage. He's a Greek, even if slightly watered down like us. He'll know what's good for you, and marriage to me would see you secure for life.'

He was a monster. He had covered every conceivable angle, and she was beginning to feel more and more trapped. She hadn't thought it possible for her hatred to grow, but it did now. 'You think you're so clever, don't you?'

A strange look crossed his face as he stood up, smoothing down his suit. 'Do I? You'd be amazed at how often I've called myself a fool, Alix. But I've nothing to lose this time,' he vouchsafed obliquely.

Alix didn't understand him, and had absolutely no wish to. 'Except a very great deal of money!'

Reaching across the desk, he ran one finger tantalisingly over her quivering lips. 'Money isn't everything. I learnt that a long time ago. As for this, I'm not taking your no for an answer. Think about it, Alix. Talk to your father if you must. I'll give you twenty-four hours. If you need to reach me, I'm staying at the Savoy.'

Alix didn't say a word, merely sat like a frozen statue and watched him leave. The soft closing of the door made her flinch, and she shuddered, lowering lids over smarting eyes. Marry Pierce? Dear God, how could she possibly accept such an offer? It was unthinkable. And yet what choice did she have? Could she really stand by and watch all her father had worked for go down the drain? Could she live with herself afterwards, knowing she had had the means to prevent it?

She shivered, feeling chilled to her bones. Marry Pierce? Resting her elbows on the desk, she sank her head on to her hands. Five years ago he had killed her with his cruelty. How could she put herself in his hands again? What was she to do? What on earth was she to do?

At three o'clock that afternoon, Alix gave up all attempts to work. Her brain simply wouldn't function, even on the simplest of matters, and her meeting with the union representative had been a confrontation she could have done without. When he had finally departed, she had felt drained. Pierce's offer filled her thoughts to the exclusion of everything else, but she knew she would never be able to rest until the matter was settled. There seemed to her to be only one way of doing that.

Collecting her briefcase and handbag, she left her office and halted by her secretary's desk. 'I'm going to visit my father, Ruth. There's something important I have to discuss with him.'

Ruth looked slightly crestfallen. 'Didn't Mr Martineau make you an offer you couldn't refuse?' she quipped.

Alix pulled a wry face at the very apt pun. 'That's what I'm afraid of. I'll see you tomorrow.' She left, very much aware that Ruth was staring at her retreating back in perplexity. However, she didn't have time to explain, even if she had felt capable of it, which she didn't.

The traffic was horrendously snarled, but at least it gave her brain a rest tackling it. None the less, she was still very hot and bothered by the time she parked her car in the hospital car park. Her father had the use of a private room, so there were no restrictions on visiting. Alix wasn't surprised to find her mother there too when she walked in, still knitting away while her husband slept.

'Have you been here all night?' Alix reproved in fond exasperation after they had greeted each other with a kiss.

'Not all night. You know they've let me use one of the rooms to sleep in, Alix,' Emily Petrakos explained, with that kind of mild determination which was hard to fight.

Realising it, Alix sighed. 'Look, I'll sit with Dad for a while. Why don't you go out for a breath of fresh air? There's a lovely day outside, and you're missing it. The change will do you good.'

'Well, if you're sure, dear,' her mother said hesitantly. 'I must admit there are some things I have to get. It's silly, I know, but I can't bear leaving him. I get the awful feeling something will happen while I'm away,' she admitted, and Alix gave her a squeeze.

'I understand, but I'll be here. So off you go,' she chivvied, relieving her parent of her knitting before helping her into her jacket and from the room, a fond smile hovering about her lips. Only then did she turn to the bed again, taking the empty seat and drawing it a little closer to the sleeping figure.

Though she needed to talk to him, she couldn't wake him. She would just have to wait until he stirred. Unfortunately, that merely left her with more time for thought. There had been no such delay when she had gone to see her grandfather five years ago, although, at that time of night, he had been in bed too. Then the catalyst had been the same as now: Pierce Martineau. She had gone reluctantly, unwilling to believe a word Pierce had said...

Yannis Petrakos came from the bedroom of his Manhattan apartment, still in the process of tying the belt of an exotic silk dressing-gown around his portly frame. His manifest irritation at being disturbed turned to surprise as he saw his granddaughter hovering by one of his Louis Quinze chairs.

'Alix? What goes on?' His frowning glance scythed between her and Pierce who stood beside her. 'Who is this man?'

Before Alix could form an answer, Pierce spoke up. 'Allow me to introduce myself,' he drawled mockingly, paying only lip-service to the usual courtesies. 'My name is Pierce Martineau, and I am Alix's husband.'

Yannis Petrakos looked pole-axed. 'Her husband? Why wasn't I informed?' he demanded in an impressive explosion of injured pride, which only served to curl Pierce's lips even more.

'We're informing you now,' he said shortly, causing the older man to stare at him intently, eyes narrowing as his brain began to tick over.

'Martineau? The name is familiar. Have we met?'

'Not directly. I made you an offer for the Petrakos shipping line. You refused.'

Her grandfather's frown deepened at the sardonic comment. He was unused to meeting people who were patently unimpressed by his presence. 'Ah, yes. I remember now. You were very persuasive, but the line has never been, nor ever will be, for sale.' The matter was closed as far as he was concerned, and as suddenly as his frown had appeared he smiled and held his hands out to Alix. 'But what has this to do with your marriage? You're a bad girl not to have told your grandpa, but I cannot be angry with you on this day of days. Come, let me kiss you. We should celebrate.'

Pierce sent Alix, who was reluctantly suffering an effusive embrace, a mocking smile. 'I wouldn't send for the champagne just yet. I think you'll find Alix wants a divorce. Isn't that so, darling?'

Yannis's face clouded again as he took a step back from his granddaughter. 'A divorce? What foolishness is this?'

'Not foolishness. I'm prepared to give her that divorce—at a price,' Pierce countered smoothly, not in the least alarmed by the older man's huffing and puffing. 'Providing you meet my price, I won't contest. However, should you fail to do so, I promise you, I could tie you up in litigation for years.'

That sent her grandfather's head back in outrage, and he drew Alix protectively to his side. 'What kind of man are you? You marry my granddaughter only to divorce her?'

Pierce smiled, eyebrow quirked mockingly, as he received the opening he had been hoping for. 'I'm a Greek by blood. And by that same blood I want revenge for my family. I want back what you stole from us, Yannis Petrakos, and in return I give you your granddaughter.'

For the first time since she entered the apartment Alix found the strength to speak. 'Grandfather, he wants Petrakos Shipping,' she declared in a choked voice. 'That's why he married me. He said you stole it, and——'

The change that came over Yannis Petrakos was a surprise to Alix, but Pierce looked as though he had expected no less. 'Quiet!' he ordered, cutting her off so harshly that she gasped. His eyes remained fixed on the younger man ranged opposite him. 'Who are you?'

'Haven't you guessed yet?' Pierce taunted. 'I am the grandson of George Andreas, and I've come to claim that which was ours,' he answered, with a natural majesty which, hate him though she did, Alix could only watch with awe. Somehow he dominated the room, and the figure of her grandfather.

The older man returned the words with a fine scorn, his accent becoming more pronounced. 'You are a fool, and the spawn of a fool. I, Yannis Petrakos, am not such a one. The document signing the ships over to me was legal and binding. Those ships are mine by law, and what is mine I keep!' In the same breath he drew Alix tightly to his side. 'And now you have brought my granddaughter to me I will not let her go. Never will I allow an Andreas to sully a Petrakos! The marriage will be annulled, and you will get nothing!'

Alix stiffened, knowing then the exact nature of the ace Pierce had up his sleeve. Words choked in her throat, and she could only stare at him in horror.

Pierce, for his part, gave her one long look, then turned all his attention on his enemy. 'The marriage cannot be annulled. I'm afraid you're too late, Petrakos. Alix and I were married yesterday. She spent the night in my bed, and gave every appearance of enjoying it,' he revealed in a voice devoid of all emotion.

Alix had thought she had plumbed the depths of humiliation today, but Pierce managed in that one brief statement to show her that the pit she was in was fathomless. She felt the tension that swamped her grandfather, and looked up to meet his accusing eyes.

'Tell me it is not so,' he demanded. 'Tell me, Alix, that you have not shamed us by lying with an Andreas.'

She had always known her grandfather was a very proud man, but had never expected to be accused of shaming the family. He made what she and Pierce had shared seem dirty, when she had slept with him out of love, and in good faith. Yet she knew it would be useless to admit that she had been ignorant of who Pierce was. It was the act, not the knowledge, that counted. The damage had been done.

All she could do was turn her anger on the man responsible for all of this. 'I cannot,' she admitted, and even as she spoke her eyes were transmitting her hatred and loathing to her husband.

There followed a long torrent of Greek which she didn't understand, but which Pierce apparently did, for he stiffened angrily, using his own knowledge of the language sparingly but with great effect. Her grandfather fell silent, although the look he sent her was chilling. Alix had the strangest feeling that Pierce had been defending her, but she couldn't imagine why he should. She glanced at him, but there was nothing to be read in his granite-like features. She decided she must have been mistaken, and was surprised to feel a stomach-twisting wave of disappointment. Which had to be the craziest thing ever, when he had used her so cruelly.

A moment later, her grandfather began speaking again, only in English this time. 'You are a clever man, Mr Martineau. You knew the one thing that would compel me to agree to your demands. You may have won, but I have a few conditions of my own. I will arrange for the divorce, and this marriage will be as if it had never existed. Neither you nor my granddaughter will ever mention it to anyone, not even your family. Should I ever hear that you have done so, then I have it in my power to make you extremely sorry.'

Pierce looked down his straight nose. 'Save your threats, Petrakos, for those you can scare. All I want is what rightfully belongs to me. The matter can be settled here and now. I know you always travel with your lawyer. Have him draw up the document tonight, and by morning I will be out of your life.'

And that was how Alix's brief marriage had ended, in the small hours of the night, by the signing of a document that bartered her for a shipping company.

Pierce had come to her before he left. A nerve had ticked in his jaw as he looked into her pale face. 'I regret that it had to be this way.'

The scorn in her eyes told him she didn't believe him. 'I don't expect it will keep you awake nights. I hope you find it's all been worth it, Pierce, that your sordid piece of paper brings you joy. But if it doesn't, you can be sure the laughter you hear will be mine!' was all she had been able to bring herself to say. She had turned away, and he had gone...she hadn't seen him again until yesterday.

Her grandfather had never forgiven her for causing him to lose his pride and joy, and had died a few years later. But she had kept her part of the bargain and never spoken of her marriage to Pierce. It had been a part of her life which she had been only too happy to forget—although she never really had forgotten. And now Pierce had come back, with another of his deals, and she felt just as trapped as she had before.

CHAPTER FIVE

ALIX was still brooding on Pierce's sudden re-appearance in her life when a sigh from the bed brought her head round swiftly, to find her father watching her.

'You were a long way away, Alix, and your thoughts didn't seem happy,' he said in a voice still distressingly lacking in power.

She rose to kiss his cheek, then perched herself on the edge of the bed, holding his hand. 'Hospitals tend to make me think negative thoughts, I'm afraid. How are you feeling? Honestly,' she added warningly.

Stephen Petrakos chuckled and smiled at his only child. 'All the better for seeing you, but not too pleased to see you frowning.' His smile faded, eyes clouding with concern and self-reproach. 'I should never have left you to deal with the mess I made! Curse it, why did I have to get ill now? The last place I need to be is tied to a hospital bed!' he exclaimed in frustration.

Alix felt her heart sink as she watched him, knowing it was bad for him to get worked up like this. 'Calm down, Dad. You won't be helping anyone if you make yourself ill again. Besides...' She bit her lip, hesitating over what to say, and how to say it. Honesty forced her to admit that a great portion of her hesitation was due to the fact that she was afraid to hear the answer.

'Besides what? Besides nobody will lift a finger to help you?' her father continued angrily, before collapsing weakly back against his pillows.

Really alarmed now, Alix quickly took the only way she knew to calm him down. 'Actually, that's not true,' she denied, and was relieved not only to see the high colour fade from his cheeks, but the reappearance of that sharpness of eye which had been a byword.

'What do you mean, Alix?'

Now she had begun, she knew she had to go on, but choose her words very carefully. She licked dry lips before plunging in the deep end. 'Well, someone does want to help, but his offer is ... unusual.' And that had to be the understatement of the year.

Her father was instantly intrigued. 'Unusual, you say? In what way, precisely? After all, we've got problems now, but basically we were a good company. We can be that way again if we can make good my mistakes. I'd assume anyone willing to inject cash would want shares in the company, and some control over what happens.' Catching sight of the wooden set of her face, he did a rapid rethink. 'You're not trying to tell me someone wants to take over completely?'

Knowing how this was her father's worst nightmare, Alix quickly reassured him. 'Not at all. In fact, quite the opposite. The thing is, there's a man who ... wants to marry me. He knows about our troubles, and he's willing to help you financially, but ... there is a problem. His name is Pierce Martineau.' She said his name quickly, then tensed, waiting for the bomb to drop. Only it never landed.

For a moment her father was speechless, then words fell over themselves in their rush to get out. 'You mean the same Martineau who's a multimillionaire?' he queried, visibly brightening. 'You call that a problem?'

Alix almost gasped herself, because she hadn't realised Pierce was that wealthy. Which made her wonder why, when he could buy anything he wanted, he should choose to help her father for no visible advantage. 'There's something else. His grandfather was George Andreas.' She dropped the name into the pool and waited for the ripples to widen. She didn't have to wait long.

Stephen Petrakos pulled a long face. 'Ah, the man my father loved to hate. I never told you about this, Alix, but the reason your grandfather and I fell out was over Andreas. He tried to make me join in the feud too, something about some ships, but I refused. That's when I came back to England and started my own company. So you see, darling, I bear no ill will towards the Andreas family. Now you say the grandson wants to marry you, and help me out of a tight spot?' Her father sat up, a broad smile spreading across his face. 'Good lord, that's the best news you could possibly have brought me. Why on earth should you think there would be a problem? I couldn't think of a better marriage for you. Have you known him long?' It was a measure of his love for her that his first thoughts were for her happiness, and not the saving of his company.

Alix had to swallow a huge lump which blocked her throat before she could answer. This was not the re-action she had wanted, and she knew now that she had hoped her father would give a flat refusal. He hadn't, and by doing so had proved Pierce right at the same time. On the face of that, it was hard to sound enthusiastic, but she did her best, albeit stiltedly.

'I . . . first met him some years ago. We went out, but nothing came of it.' She nearly choked on the downright lie, and cleared her throat before continuing. 'Then he turned up at the function last night, and...'

'He told you how he hadn't forgotten you in all those years, and asked you to marry him? So that's what your mother meant when she told me you might have some good news!'

Alix glanced down at her fingers, which were tying themselves in knots. Trust her father, the ultimate romantic, to see it all through rose-coloured glasses. 'You don't think it was rather too sudden?'

'Nonsense. When a man sees what he wants, he goes for it! Why should he wait? And why should he not want to marry you? You're beautiful and intelligent, the perfect wife for any man. What could be better?'

Her heart sank even further. She gave him a wry smile. 'You haven't asked me if I love him, Dad.'

He waved a dismissive hand. 'If you don't love him now, you'll grow to. I've been concerned about you, darling. What would happen to you if I weren't here? This marriage will stop me worrying.' Impulsively he squeezed her hand. 'There are worse things than arranged marriages, Alix. Your mother and I had one, and it couldn't have been happier. You just have to learn to give and take.'

She knew that to her cost, but in her experience some took more than they gave. However, she kept her own counsel. Nor did she tell her father that she hadn't said yes yet. The difference her news had made on him was proof enough that there was only one course open to her. Inwardly fuming at the trap which had closed so firmly around her, she put on a brave face and smiled.

'You'd better wish me happy, then. And this time when I tell you to stop worrying you'll know that you can, hmm?'

Her father laughed, and was still chuckling when her mother came back. Of course, the news had to be broken to her, and she wept with mingled relief for her husband and joy for her daughter. Alix found herself having to promise to bring Pierce to meet them, a prospect that strained her smile to its limit. When she eventually left, half an hour later, she felt emotionally drained by the need to keep up the pretence, and the knowledge that the eventful day was still very far from over. There was Pierce to see.

Of course, she could have put the meeting off until tomorrow, but it would not have been any easier. Experience had taught her that it was better to take bad medicine quickly. Get the worst over with.

She drove herself to the Savoy in a mood of fomenting anger. She had hoped, when their divorce had been made final, that she would never see Pierce again, but now she was going to have to tie herself to him for the rest of her life. For that had been his offer, and it wasn't negotiable. The money was only available in exchange for her becoming his wife again, and there was no prospect of divorce. The thought brought a sharp stab of pain to her temple.

She hated being trapped this way, but what she really couldn't understand was why Pierce should want her as his wife when he surely knew how she felt about him. Nor was she stupid enough to imagine his offer was in any way altruistic. There had to be something else behind the move, something other than merely helping her father out of trouble. He was an extremely handsome and extremely wealthy man, and could have had any woman he wanted as his wife, so why tie himself to someone who hated him?

The question was still uppermost in her mind when she entered the hotel and had the desk clerk ring Pierce's suite. Her last hope, that he wouldn't be in, was squashed when she was told to go straight up. In the lift, she checked her appearance in the mirror. Her suit no longer looked as fresh as it had, and her make-up was decidedly tired. A swift application of lipstick and the running of a brush through her hair at least made her feel more presentable. She supposed she should have gone home and changed first, but the need to get the meeting over with had been too compelling.

Her knock was answered by Pierce himself, looking very relaxed with his tie removed and a couple of buttons undone, and his shirt-sleeves rolled up to reveal strong tanned forearms liberally sprinkled with dark hairs. He didn't bother to ask why she was there, merely stood back to allow her to enter, closing the door with a firm click behind them. To Alix it felt as if the last means of escape had been removed, and a sense of impotent anger had her walking forward to drop her handbag on to the nearest coffee-table. Pierce followed her. She could feel his eyes on her back, and imagined him laughing at her, a sense so strong that she swung round, only to discover she was wrong. His eyes were hooded, watchful, a light-year away from mockery.

Confused and annoyed, she tossed her head. 'I've just come from the hospital,' she informed him bluntly, and the watchfulness sharpened intensely.

'How is your father?'

She sighed in frustration, lips twisting with self-mockery as she raked a hand through her short blonde locks, combing them into delightful disarray. 'Making a rapid recovery. You'll be pleased to know that he himself bears no grudge to any member of the Andreas family.'

'Unlike his daughter,' Pierce observed drily, and walked over to where a tray of drinks stood on a sideboard. 'Can I get you something? You look as if you could do with it.'

The shirt stretched taut over his muscles as he fiddled with bottles and glasses, and she stared at his broad back, wishing she didn't instantly remember how his flesh had felt beneath her hands. Yet she only had to be near him to experience such vivid mental pictures, and in a desperate attempt at self-preservation she hastily brought a shutter down on the memories. 'I'll have a Scotch,' she said tersely, and raised her chin as he looked round at her in surprise. Her smile was saccharine-sweet. 'They say it has anaesthetic qualities, which I'll need if I have to spend any length of time with you. I shouldn't be surprised if I spend my days in an alcoholic mist.'

He didn't find that at all amusing, but she didn't see why she should consider his feelings when he had never given a thought for hers. Nor did it surprise her that the glass he eventually handed her held only white wine. The whisky he had himself, swallowing half the contents of his glass at one go, while Alix felt her eyes drawn irresistibly to his tanned throat. A dull flush crept from her neck into her cheeks, and she hastily turned away, hating herself for the wantonness of her thoughts and the reaction of her body. He hadn't touched her, yet her flesh had quickened, her breasts swelling to push against her clothing, making her feel achingly restricted. It was intolerable to feel so weak-willed, and, unable to remain still, she went and stood at the window, tensing as Pierce's reflection came to join hers.

'From your reaction, I take it you told him about my offer, and he didn't throw it out?' he mused idly, and she laughed bitterly.

'You knew he wouldn't. That's why you told me to speak to him. You knew I wanted him to back me up, too. God, it must be wonderful to be male, and right all the time!' she jeered, hating him, wishing he would move away so that she wouldn't feel the heat and smell the scent of him. It was a combination designed to make her so very much aware of him.

If he received the unspoken message, he ignored it. 'If I thought you really believed that, I'd give you an argument. You're just angry that you have no reason to refuse my offer,' he said reasonably, and it made her so angry that she turned on him.

'Wrong! I have every reason to refuse you. My father might think you're the best thing since sliced bread, but I know better, don't I? He has nothing against arranged marriages either, which is just as well, because there's no one better than you at arranging them to suit yourself!' she riposted scornfully, hoping to wither him, but knowing her chances were slim.

Pierce stared down into her animated face, inspecting each feature separately, as if, for obscure reasons of his own, he was committing them to memory. 'You're very beautiful. In fact, you're still the most beautiful woman I've ever seen,' he informed her gently, completely taking the wind out of her sails.

'What?' Her eyes widened in confusion, a reaction which brought a faint smile to twist his lips.

'I was paying you a compliment.'

Alix shook her head, rallying defences which had been neatly side-stepped. 'Well, don't waste your time. You don't have to win me over with empty words. You already hold all the cards. I don't suppose you even thought for a minute that I'd say no. I love my father too much to reject the only offer he's had, however much I would like to,' she sniped, allowing all the resentment she felt to spill out.

Pierce took a deep breath, jaw flexing. 'Our marriage doesn't have to be a battlefield, Alix,' he said tersely, revealing that perhaps there was more tension in him than was obvious to the naked eye.

'As far as I'm concerned, it can be nothing else,' she rejected. 'Or did you imagine you were getting the same naïve fool as before? That person no longer exists. You destroyed her, Pierce. You'll be getting me, as I am, and if you don't like it then you've only yourself to blame. Is that clear enough for you?'

Taking his time, Pierce drained his glass and set it aside. When he next gave her his full attention, his eyes were steely. 'You've made yourself more than clear. However, if you imagined that by declaring your dislike of me and the arrangement it would induce me to change my terms, then you were mistaken. You'll be my wife, in every sense of the word.'

Alix gritted her teeth, making herself return his stare with all the disdain she could muster. 'I wouldn't dream of refusing. After all, it's a matter of honour. You'll be buying the rights to me, won't you? But there's just one thing you've miscalculated—I don't have to enjoy it.'

Unfortunately that only served to bring a wicked gleam to his eyes, and he moved a step closer. 'Are you suggesting you won't? Now *that's* a very naïve statement. I have a very vivid memory of how whole-heartedly you throw yourself into making love,' he purred dangerously, making the fine hairs rise all over her skin.

Dear God, how dared he say such things? 'That was before I learned to hate you,' she retorted witheringly, then gasped as his hands came out to fasten on her shoulders, drawing her inexorably towards him. 'Let me go, Pierce. Damn you, I said let me go!' she ordered, struggling to break free but failing miserably, because he was, and always had been, far too strong for her. All too aware of her many weaknesses where he was concerned, she lifted her gaze to his face, and there was a look of intent in his eye which set her heart thudding wildly.

'When I'm ready,' he gritted out as he managed to subdue her, fastening both her hands behind her back with just one of his. The other he used to frame her face and turn her head up. 'After all, you've just got through telling me I've bought you, so I can do pretty much as I like—can't I, darling?' he taunted, and brought his mouth down on hers.

And, like before, it was no assault but a calculated seduction of her senses, tasting her lips with his tongue, drawing the sensual fullness of her lower lip into his mouth and stroking the silky inner skin until she shivered helplessly. It made no difference that she kept her teeth clenched against him. He teased her until she could no longer withhold a gasp of pleasure, and then took possession without a fight, tantalising her with the erotic stroking of his tongue on hers.

She didn't want to respond, but couldn't help herself against his powerful magic and the swift arousal of her body. Even as one small part of her brain was calling her a fool she returned his kiss feverishly. She was scarcely aware of him releasing the buttons of her jacket and pushing it aside to claim one thrusting breast, teasing her nipple into an aching point which sent a shaft of pleasure deep to the core of her. When his mouth left hers, she was trembling in every limb, and when her breast was sucked into the moist cavern of his mouth her head fell back, and she groaned aloud as her body went into spasm.

Dazedly, her eyes focused on the ceiling. Her hands were free, but she could only use them to cling on to his shoulders as the world tilted. Then, suddenly, it righted itself again, and there was Pierce looking down at her speculatively. In an instant the heat vanished, leaving her chilled and abandoned, with only an overwhelming self-disgust for company.

'It looks as if our wedding night is going to be very interesting,' Pierce declared with heavy irony. 'Your hatred seems to add a certain spice to the proceedings.' He steadied her before letting her go, retrieving his glass and crossing the room to refill it.

Alix dropped her head, but that only brought to her gaze the damp silk of her camisole, which clung to her aroused flesh like a second skin. Sickened by the evidence of her own weakness, she pulled her jacket closed, but her fingers shook terribly as she struggled with the buttons. When she finished, she looked up to find Pierce watching her over the rim of his glass. She froze, pained colour washing into her cheeks. Unable to find anything to say that would drop him where he stood, she waited for him to speak, tensing to bow with his scorn.

'Have you eaten?'

The prosaic question wasn't what she expected at all. 'No,' she answered honestly, albeit huskily, wondering why he had chosen not to go on with his advantage.

'I'll have something sent up,' Pierce decided, reaching for the telephone. 'We have things to discuss, and I have no wish to do so in public. Do you agree?'

'Do I have a choice?' Alix queried caustically, struggling to find a measure of composure which could match his.

Even across the room she could see him stiffen angrily. 'Of course you have a choice. I'm not a monster, you know,' he told her shortly, then had to alter his tone as Room Service answered and he had to give his attention to ordering the food.

For her part, Alix didn't care what he ordered, as she doubted if she'd be able to eat a thing. She crossed to the nearest chair and sank into it gratefully. She felt deathly tired, emotionally drained, and let her head fall back against the cushioned back, closing her eyes. What she would give to be able not to think! She'd give ten times as much not to feel this attraction for Pierce. She had believed it dead, but the instant she had seen him again her senses had become vitally alive. Even now her body throbbed from the cessation of his lovemaking, making a mockery of her belief that she had forgotten him.

Nothing was forgotten, but passion would blank her mind temporarily. Was that how he expected to keep her under control? By allowing the mindlessness of their nights to make up for the hatred of the days? It was a thought which brought a spark of rebellion flickering into life. He might want it so, but it didn't have to be. She didn't have to give in without a fight. He had said as much himself, when he had asked what better way was there for her to get her revenge than to marry him. She had dismissed it then, but now the idea took hold. She might not be able to get out of this marriage, but she didn't have to be the biddable little wife! After all, she wasn't defenceless; a woman had weapons of her own. And even if she didn't win the war she could make good and sure he had to win a lot of battles to gain his victory!

That brought a smile to her lips, returning some of her lost energy, and she opened her eyes again, only to find Pierce watching her, eyes gleaming with some inner amusement.

'Plotting my downfall?'

Her nerves jolted violently at the idea that he could read her mind, and there was no way she could halt the flush that stole revealingly into her cheeks. All she could do was brazen it out. 'Why shouldn't I? I did learn something from our first marriage, short as it was—you can achieve almost anything with forward planning.'

Pierce slipped his hands into his trouser pockets and rocked back on his heels. 'So you're planning to use me as your role model?'

Alix produced an insouciant shrug. 'Why bother to look around for someone else when I have my very own master to hand, so to speak?'

'You never used to be so cynical. I remember you viewing the world with an open-minded *joie de vivre*,' he mused broodingly.

She laughed at that, for he almost sounded disappointed. 'Ah, well, they do say marriage can be a real eye-opener, and mine, you'll admit, was a real lulu!'

Pierce shook his head, a soft laugh escaping him although it contained little humour, more like derision. 'You're never going to forgive me for that, are you?' It was a statement, not a question, and Alix sent him a look of scorn.

'If that's what you want, you'll have a very long wait. In fact, if I were you, I'd give serious thought to the possibility of reincarnation, because there will be no absolution from me in this lifetime!' Alix informed him bluntly, allowing her eyes to flash her dislike to him in semaphore.

To her aggravation, Pierce didn't get angry, just more thoughtful. 'I rather like the idea of us going down the centuries together. Always together,' he repeated mockingly, savouring the words.

Alix snapped her fingers in irritation. 'Don't sound so smug. Nothing says we have to come back as humans. If there was any justice, you'd come back as a bug that I could crush under my foot!' she declared acridly, and had the annoying sight of Pierce bursting into a laugh of real amusement. Her heart kicked in her chest, and the years seemed to fall from him, making him more the man she had first met, and she realised there was a sternness in him now, a damping down of that vital spark which had first drawn her to him. It saddened her to think of its loss. But almost immediately she called herself a fool for being so sentimental. Pierce wasn't, and she couldn't afford to be.

'I'm so glad I amuse you,' she said blightingly, and he grinned at her.

'Oh, you do more than that, darling,' he told her softly, and the heat in his eyes sent her a message she had no trouble interpreting. The attraction was mutual. She aroused him just as much as he aroused her, and the knowledge had her loins clenching on a fierce wave of desire. A need she rejected fiercely.

'If you could manage to drag your mind from the gutter, you said we had business to discuss,' she said with patent distaste, which unfortunately only had him crossing to her in that languid stride of his which hinted at a barely leashed animal power.

Bending, he took her chin between his thumb and finger. 'So I did, but don't sound so high and mighty, Alix. We both know that it wouldn't take very much effort on my part to get you down into the gutter with me, so caught up in your own passion that you wouldn't care where you were so long as I gave you the satisfaction you craved,' he taunted silkily, making her colour fluctuate wildly and her mouth go dry.

Her grey eyes glittered with proud tears. 'You're a——'

'Heartless swine,' he finished for her. 'I know, and it will be easier for you if you remember it, if you want to keep your precious pride intact.'

Even had Alix been able to find a reply there was no opportunity to say it, for they were interrupted by a knock on the door. Pierce straightened with a wry smile.

'Saved by the dinner bell!' he gibed, and went to answer it, leaving Alix sitting trembling in her chair.

Dear God, how on earth could she live with him? she thought angrily, then her shoulders slumped. How could she not? She had no choice. When it came to Pierce Martineau, she never had.

CHAPTER SIX

Two days later, Alix arrived at her office feeling very much as if she had been run over by a steamroller. Having elicited her acceptance of his proposal, Pierce had moved with what, in other circumstances, would have been called commendable speed. She could only see it as unseemly haste, and resented being carried along in his slipstream.

Pouring herself a cup of coffee from the pot which was always kept hot, she stood staring out of the window, trying not to feel as if everything was getting way out of her control. She wondered what shocks were in store for her today. Yesterday morning Pierce had insisted on going with her to the hospital to meet her parents. To her chagrin, he had made an instant hit with them. Yet, despite her feelings of anger, she hadn't been able to help but admire the way he'd handled the situation, and she'd found herself awarding him her grudging appreciation.

Even as he had enlarged on his proposals for saving the business he had deferred to her father. Only with his agreement would a manager be installed to supervise the company until Stephen was well enough to return. Neither would the results of the report compiled by Pierce's management team into ways of streamlining and improving production be implemented without her father's full agreement. Which, naturally, he had got, along with Stephen Petrakos's undisguised respect.

The only thing to mar the occasion had been her father's insistence that Pierce had to be in love with his daughter to be so generous. A fact the younger man did nothing to deny, instead giving credibility to it by slipping his arm around her and keeping it there despite her surreptitious, but determined, efforts to shake it off. When they had eventually departed, she had been left with the unpalatable fact that he had quite won them over. And, although she understood that it had been a deliberate ploy to ease any worries they might have had, she bitterly resented him for it.

Heaving a deep sigh, she sat down at her desk and reached for her mail, surprised to find that the top envelope simply had her name written on it. Frowning, she opened it, spreading out the single sheet of paper it contained. There were only a few words on the page, but they sent her into a white-hot fury. It was from Pierce, detailing the date, time and place of their wedding. Innocent enough in itself, except that he had sent it to her in a memo! He had actually had the gall to reduce an act which was going to change her life to a bit of business!

So angry that she was shaking, she was just about to snatch up the telephone in order to ring him at his hotel and give him a piece of her mind when she heard the phone ring in her father's office. Puzzled, because all calls had been routed to her for the last few weeks, she had half risen to go and answer it when the ringing ceased and she heard the muffled sound of someone speaking.

Even as she crossed the room to investigate she had a premonition of what she would find. When she thrust open the connecting door, it came as no surprise to see Pierce sitting in her father's chair, calmly carrying on a telephone conversation. Catching sight of her, he indicated that she should take a seat, but that only served to infuriate her further, and she ignored him, choosing instead to send him a glare which didn't go halfway to showing him how she was feeling.

Pierce didn't hurry himself. It was a good five minutes before he put the receiver down and turned to face her, by which time she was ready to explode.

'What are *you* doing here? How dare you think you can simply walk into my father's office and take it over?' she challenged with icy anger. He might think he could take over her life, but that was all.

Pierce sank back in the leather chair and regarded her mockingly. 'For your information, darling, I didn't "think" I could do anything—I knew. When I went to see Stephen last night, he suggested that I use his office in order to facilitate the plans I had drawn up. I accepted.'

Brought up short, Alix swallowed back any further words she had had ready and channelled her anger along another course. 'Why wasn't I told? I suppose, now that you're in charge, I don't count! If you didn't feel up to telling me to my face, then the very least you could have done was send me a memo!' she rejoined tartly, and very much to the point.

At that, Pierce raised his brows in sudden comprehension, then ran a finger thoughtfully along the side of his nose. 'Ah.'

It took just that one sound to make her realise that she'd lost ground rather than gaining it. She made a despairing noise in her throat and turned her back on him, pacing away. 'I do not appreciate being treated like some damned afterthought!'

'As the central character, you were hardly that,' he returned, not troubling to hide his amusement. 'However, I was under the impression—and correct me if I'm wrong—that you wanted everything to be kept on a business footing.'

Damn him, he was always turning the tables by using her own words against her! Cursing herself, she swung round again. 'Much you care about what I want, Pierce Martineau. And as for keeping everything businesslike, how do you explain why yesterday you were at pains to pretend you were in love with me? We both know it was a lie, although I have to admit it wasn't up to your usual standard of deceit.'

Pierce never took his eyes off her as she paced the floor. 'Your parents believed it, and that was the object of the exercise. Or are you suggesting I should have told them the barefaced truth rather than an acceptable lie?'

'Even you wouldn't have the bad taste to tell them you were getting my body in return for services rendered,' she sneered.

He was on his feet in an instant, every step he took towards her brimming over with barely leashed fury. 'You push your luck to the very limit, don't you, Alix? Just what is it you're trying to make me do? Get so angry that I'll take you by force? So that then you will always be able to claim you had no choice? Is that what you really want to happen?'

Reeling from the waves of violent emotion coming at her, Alix stared at him through stormy eyes. Her heart quailed. She had never seen him this angry before, and she knew she was to blame. There was some devil inside her that kept her pushing and pushing. So was there any wonder that he had finally reacted? It was time for a tactical retreat. 'No,' she admitted gruffly, and was relieved to see him take a deep breath.

'Then you'd better walk easy around me, darling, and learn where to draw the line. I'm prepared to give you a certain amount of leeway, but push me too far and you'll have to take the consequences.' He turned away from her then, raking a hand through his hair as he returned to stand by the desk. Picking something up from the surface, he held it out to her. 'These are for you.'

Gathering up her badly shaken composure, Alix went to him, taking the folder he offered quickly, as if he were a snake ready to strike. Inside were credit cards for certain well-known stores, and she glanced up at him in quick enquiry.

'You'll need a trousseau. You'd better take the afternoon off and go shopping,' he suggested evenly, turning his attention to the papers on the desk as if the subject was now closed.

If he had his limits, then so did she. He might have bought her, but she'd be damned if she'd be kept! 'I don't need you to buy me clothes, Pierce. I have an adequate salary of my own, and besides, I don't need any new clothes,' Alix pointed out tersely.

Glancing up, Pierce shook his head slowly. 'You know, it would be a delightful change if you'd just do as you're told for once. However, I can see you're determined to fight me on everything, aren't you? Unfortunately for you I am equally determined. I don't care how many clothes you have, Alix. In my experience a woman can always find room for more, just as you're going to do.'

It was a battle of wills, and right then his was stronger. 'If it means that much to you, then I'm surprised you don't insist on coming with me,' she challenged, with something that was very nearly a flounce. The child-ishness of that brought her up short, and she realised she was allowing him to make her act totally out of character.

Pierce, on the other hand, was the epitome of calm assurance and control. 'Believe me, I would, if only I weren't so busy saving your father's company from bankruptcy,' he drawled, scoring a direct hit.

Inwardly she reeled from a reminder she really didn't need. Ambivalently, she knew she should be grateful, but he made her so angry all the time that that emotion swamped everything else. Common sense returning, she decided there was more than one way to skin a cat, and, to mix metaphors, he might insist on leading her to water, but he couldn't make her drink. Taking the cards didn't mean she intended to comply with his edict. Armed by the idea of outsmarting him, she simply couldn't resist salaaming. 'To hear is to obey, o master.'

However, instead of angering him it seemed to restore his sense of humour, for he eyed her in distinct amusement. 'Anyone less like a willing slave I'd be hard pressed to find. And when I come to think of it I wouldn't want you any other way than as you are. It makes every encounter that much more of an adventure.'

Alix frowned at him. 'How can it be, when you've already...?' The words tailed off and she felt a soft flush invade her cheeks.

'Already had you?' he supplied for her, in a voice as smooth as dark chocolate. 'True, but you loved me then, and you don't now,' he pointed out next, and the heat left her cheeks, leaving them waxen.

'I don't think I could ever have loved you,' she told him flatly, walking over to the door.

Pierce leant against the desk and folded his arms. 'If you didn't, you couldn't have hated me so much, and for so long. But who's to say where love ends and hate begins? You've never forgotten me, the same as I never forgot you. That spark is still there between us, however much you might wish it wasn't.'

Clutching hold of the door-handle, Alix threw him a stormy glance. 'Sex isn't love, Pierce. You taught me that. Now I know the difference, I'm never going to mistake a sham for the real thing.'

If he was meant to feel ashamed, he gave no sign of it. 'I'm glad to hear it,' he said drily, and glanced at his watch. 'You might as well go off now. And don't imagine that you can get away with simply disappearing for the afternoon and only pretending to buy. I'll be calling for you at eight to take you to dinner, and I expect to see the results of your afternoon. Is that clear?'

For a moment she had the awful feeling that he could read her mind, and his gently ironic smile almost confirmed it until reason asserted itself and she acknowledged that it wasn't difficult for him to guess what she might do. Thwarted, she bit back a rash retort, and smiled. 'As if I would do such a thing!' she murmured dulcetly, and he laughed.

'Hmm, as if! Happy hunting,' he tagged on to her departing back, and Alix thought that if she only had a shotgun she knew precisely which animal she'd like to shoot and have stuffed and mounted! And then, perversely, the very idea brought a gurgle of laughter to her lips, so that she was actually smiling as she gathered up her handbag and went to tell Ruth that she wouldn't be back today.

'Well, you certainly look more cheerful,' her secretary was prompted to say, and Alix gave a wry grimace.

'Little things please little minds. Once you've done those letters, Ruth, perhaps you'd better offer your services to Mr Martineau. He'll be using my father's office for the next few days.' She was about to go when something else occurred to her. 'Oh, and if anyone wants to see me you'd better pass them on to him too. See you tomorrow.'

Once outside on the street, she decided to leave her car where it was and hail a taxi. The garage was locked overnight, so the vehicle would be perfectly safe. Allowing herself to sink back in the seat, she took out the cards, tapping them thoughtfully against her thumbnail. Her first angry reaction would have been to cut them up, but now a much better idea struck her. If Pierce wanted her to spend his money, then she would, and for once in her life she wasn't going to bother checking the price of anything she bought.

As a rule she always bought with durability and value for money in mind, thinking it less than clever to spend just because you had the money, so a wave of compunction did hit her when she saw the pile of boxes being put into the taxi after her visit to the first store. Then she took herself severely to task, for a faint heart would avail her nothing against a man as strong-willed as Pierce. She had to prove to him that she was no walk-over, and the chances to do that were proving few and far between.

When she finally went home, though, she did wonder if she had overdone it when the result of her efforts lay strewn about her, cluttering up every chair and almost all of her lounge carpet. Then she decided what the hell, she couldn't take them back, so she might just as well brazen it out. With which thought in mind, she went around opening the boxes and draping their contents hither and thither. After which she felt in need of refreshment, and made herself some tea and toast.

With Pierce expected at eight, Alix then took herself off to bathe and wash her hair, and it was while she was drying it, seated at her dressing-table, that an added refinement came to her. So that when, just before the appointed hour, the front doorbell rang, she took a deep breath and went to answer it in a stunning ankle-length designer coat in a shade of blue which deepened her grey eyes mysteriously.

Pierce, looking devastatingly handsome in an Armani dinner-suit, eyed her for a moment in silence before commenting drily, 'Does this mean you're ready to go, or that your central heating has broken down?'

Alix, trying to settle down a heart which had begun to trip along madly at the sheer power of him, shook her head and stood back to allow him to enter. A niggling doubt about what she was going to do was pushed firmly to the back of her mind. It was far too late for second thoughts. 'Neither. This coat is one of the purchases you said you wanted to see,' she informed him, walking ahead of him into the lounge. While she was conscious of him coming to a halt on the threshold, she continued into the middle of the room, where she swung to face him.

With a silent whistle, he was surveying the scene, hands slipping casually into his trouser pockets, as he raised his eyes to hers. 'Were you hoping to break the bank? If so, I should tell you this wouldn't even make a dent in it.'

'On the contrary, as you didn't set a limit, I thought I might as well indulge myself. Kit myself out from the skin, and top to toe.' With a dramatic gesture she flung her arms wide, ostensibly to indicate her purchases, and as a consequence the coat parted to reveal a glimpse of the black and red lace French corset which was all she wore underneath. 'Everything you see has been bought and paid for by you,' she declared, and quite audibly heard Pierce catch his breath.

It was the unmistakable tension in his lithe frame which made her suddenly decide she had gone too far, and the muscles of her stomach lurched with something that was half fear and half something she didn't care to put a name to. Swallowing hard, she stared at him, seeing the dull colour rise in his cheeks and the nerve begin to tick in his jaw. Very slowly his hands came out of his pockets as he straightened to his full height.

'I take it you include yourself in that statement?' he said in a strange tone of voice, pacing towards her with leonine grace. 'You've obviously laid everything out so that I might see each item, but I notice you've covered yourself up. I would hardly call that fair, would you? After all, it's only right I should see what I'm getting, I wouldn't want to buy a pig in a poke. So why don't you take the coat off, Alix?' he finished as he came to a halt a yard away.

She knew then that she had underestimated him entirely. She had intended this to be a slap in the face, but had gone in rashly without thinking of all the possible consequences. Still, rebellious in the face of attack, she wasn't about to turn tail and run, so she lifted her chin and slipped the coat off, tossing it aside. She was, after all, better clothed than if she was dressed for swimming.

Except, of course, she had chosen to wear the sexiest piece of underwear she had bought.

It was Pierce's slow perusal which brought the hot colour to her cheeks, and it took an effort to stay still and not squirm in outrage. Because his inspection was deliberately salacious. She had thrown down the gauntlet and he had picked it up. Sickening as it was, she knew she had brought it on herself, with her impetuosity, and must see it through to the bitter end.

'Turn around,' he commanded huskily, and with a choked gasp she hastily swivelled, shivering as she felt the brush of his eyes on her. 'Very nice...what I can see of you. Are you cold?' This last comment came as another shiver ran through her, which owed nothing to temperature.

'No,' she denied hoarsely, and he sighed.

'Good, because I wouldn't want you to catch a chill when you remove that last little piece of nothing you've got on,' Pierce observed mockingly.

With a gasp of horror, Alix glanced disbelievingly over her shoulder. 'Y-you can't be serious?' she stammered.

Pierce's smile was like a viper's. 'Weren't *you* serious? You said I'd bought everything I could see, and had even gone to the trouble of laying it out for my inspection.'

Alix tried desperately to laugh. 'But it was all a joke!' she protested sickly.

'Really?' Pierce challenged ironically, crossing his arms. 'Well, I don't see you laughing, Alix, and neither am I. You wanted to see me humiliated, but I've seen through your little "joke". Now it's my turn. You'd better get on with it, darling. I've a table booked for eight-thirty, and I don't want to be late.'

Feeling totally humiliated, Alix turned away, head dropping as she fought to hold back hot tears. She was the one who should have been gloating, but it had all gone miserably wrong. She looked around for escape. The bedroom wasn't far away, but she doubted very much if she'd make it, because Pierce was between her and the door. No, he'd stop her, because he meant to have his pound of flesh. The only thing she could do was get the whole stupid business over with. Choking back a sob, she moved her hands round to the back zip and began to slide it down, but halfway she was forced to stop as another sob broke free and she knew she just couldn't do it.

Behind her she heard Pierce swear under his breath, and then his fingers were brushing hers aside and closing the zip again. Then one firm hand framed her chin and brought her tear-washed gaze up to his flinty one.

'You stupid little fool. Haven't you learned yet that it doesn't pay to play games with me? Oh, go and get dressed! And you can forget about dinner; I've lost my appetite. The field is yours, Alix; I leave you in command of it. I hope the victory was worth it.'

Biting down hard on her lip, Alix watched him turn and leave, and a moment later heard the front door slam. Feeling like a fool, she stared at the scene of her humiliation. He was right, she had wanted to shame him, but it was herself who had been made to feel cheap. The clothes returned her stare with inanimate mockery. She wished she'd never seen them, and knew for a fact that she would never wear the red and black creation again.

Writhing with self-disgust, she went to take a cleansing shower, but she knew it would take more than that to wash the memory from her mind. Consequently she slept badly, tossing and turning the whole night through. It was during one of the sleepless hours that she decided she would have to apologise, however much the words might stick in her throat.

So it really wasn't surprising that she overslept, and, having done so, decided there was no need to rush. She was already late for work, so a little longer wouldn't make any difference. She used the time to force down some toast she didn't really want, and took extra care over her appearance. Wanting to look cool and self-possessed, she used make-up to mask the ravages of her sleepless night and chose a silver-grey silk suit which she teamed with a red blouse. Then, feeling like a condemned woman, she finally headed into the city.

Despite her efforts, she wasn't prepared to walk into a suspiciously busy lobby and have all eyes turn on her as silence fell. It made her want to scuttle into the lift like a crab searching for its shell, and she was afraid she had probably done so. Why on earth had everyone been grinning? It was a puzzle which deepened when she walked into her outer office and faced Ruth, who had obviously been waiting on tenterhooks for her arrival.

Smiling broadly and clutching a folded newspaper, her secretary handed over a pile of messages. 'You certainly know how to keep a secret, Alix! None of us even guessed from the way you've been acting. Congratulations, I hope you'll both be very happy.'

Rifling through the pile in astonishment, Alix glanced at her secretary in confusion. 'What are you talking about?'

'The wedding. The announcement is in all the papers,' Ruth explained, handing over her own copy. 'Didn't you know about it? Perhaps Mr Martineau wanted it to be a surprise.'

Seeing the light at last, Alix managed a smile, returning the newspaper. 'I expect so,' she declared drily, and he had certainly succeeded. In her office she glanced through the messages again, and tightened her lips. With few exceptions, they were all from people who had refused to help her only days ago. Now, with Pierce's arrival, they couldn't get in contact quickly enough. It was hard not to feel bitter, and it didn't make it any easier to enter her father's office and face Pierce.

He glanced up from a document he was studying, slowly lowering it to the desk as she came across to him. He didn't smile, but then she had hardly expected him to. 'What can I do for you, Alix?' he asked, with barely concealed impatience.

It was an attitude calculated to put her back up straight away, but she mastered her impulse to let off a vitriolic salvo. 'Why didn't you tell me about the announcement?'

Pierce sighed, sending her a quizzical look. 'Perhaps because I didn't want an argument from you. But it looks as though I'm going to get one anyway, doesn't it?'

Crossing her arms, Alix took a deep breath. First things first. 'I didn't come here to fight, Pierce, I came to apologise.' At least she had got the words out without choking.

'Now there's a novelty!' he jeered softly, and instantly her temperature rose.

'Do you want this apology or not?' she charged tartly.

One finger smoothed over his lips thoughtfully. 'Curious how it sounds more like a declaration of war.'

She flung her hands up in exasperation. 'That's because you always say something to make me mad! If you'd just be quiet for five minutes, I can have my say and go!'

Much to her surprise, he laughed. 'You'd be wasted in the diplomatic corps. OK, you have the floor, Miss Petrakos.'

Damn him! Alix thought wildly. Battling to keep her voice level, her chin rose fractionally in unconscious defiance. 'I realise the stunt I pulled last night was in bad taste. I'm sorry.'

There was a silence for several seconds before he answered. 'Is that it? Very well, apology accepted,' he acknowledged, and reached for the document again.

Alix's lips parted on a tiny gasp. 'Is that all you're going to say?' she demanded in disbelief.

Pierce looked coolly amused. 'You were maybe expecting something else?'

Her teeth came together in an audible snap. 'I thought,' she began scornfully, 'that you might want to apologise yourself.'

All amusement left him. 'For what? Beating you at your own game? Perhaps I might if I thought you wouldn't be trying something else the minute my back was turned,' he told her bluntly. 'But while you're here there are a few things you need to know. You'd better sit down.'

He was amazing! He seemed to think he could say what he liked, and then expect her to sit down for a cosy chat! 'Thanks, but I prefer to stand.'

Pierce didn't raise his voice. 'Sit down, Alix, or I'll come round there and make you.'

After last night, she decided that discretion was the better part of valour, and quickly took the seat opposite him.

He sent her a grim smile, sitting back and crossing his legs. 'Comfy? I'll try not to keep you too long. I know your time is precious. You'll be delighted to hear that after the wedding we'll be taking a short honeymoon, so you'd better arrange for leave. Also, you can get Personnel to put in an advertisement for your job. That way we'll be ready to interview as soon as we get back.'

Alix was too stunned to utter a word for a moment or two, then they spluttered out. 'What do you mean, advertise my job? I worked damn hard to get here, and I'll be damned if I give it up for you or anybody!'

'Nevertheless, the position will be vacant,' he informed her with a steely glint in his eye. 'You'll be my wife, Alix. You didn't seriously imagine you could stay here when I go home? Although I have houses in most European capitals, my home is in the States. As my wife, you'll be living there with me.'

She cursed herself for a fool then, because she hadn't actually thought of what would happen after they were married. She really should have known. 'And what about my career?' she challenged, choking on a fresh wave of bitterness.

'I'm afraid that will have to take a back seat,' Pierce replied dismissively. 'Will it really matter? I remember you telling me once that you had no intention of being a working wife.'

It was an unnecessary reminder, recalling to her her own naïveté. 'That was in another life. My career is important to me now, Pierce.'

'It won't be when you have a family of your own. Or had you forgotten that ours is to be a real marriage, darling?'

Grey eyes flashed her dislike. 'A real marriage is supposed to be a partnership! There's supposed to be mutual respect. We have neither. My only choice is to do exactly what you say, isn't it?'

'You've heard of the phrase, He who pays the piper calls the tune? So far, all the giving has been on my side,' Pierce shot back coldly, and she flinched.

'I see. You really know how to make a person hate you, don't you, Pierce? I suppose this honeymoon is where I pay back the first instalment?' she charged in a choked voice.

'Neither of us can escape our destiny, Alix,' he said evenly, and she shook her head.

'You talk as if we have no control over our lives. As if it's all been pre-ordained by some higher being. I don't believe that, and I won't give in to your belief,' she countered fiercely. How could she believe it? For it would mean there was no escape.

'Perhaps you already are,' Pierce observed wryly. 'Much as I'd like to, I really don't have time to discuss the finer philosophical points with you. My team are arriving today, and we've a hell of a lot of work to get through before the wedding. You should look to clearing your desk too.'

Dismissed, Alix said nothing, because there was absolutely nothing to say. Argument was useless. Anything she said he would ignore anyway. She merely rose and went back into her own office. An office which would not be hers for very much longer. Crossing to the window, she stared stormily out at the London land-scape. She felt as if she was being taken over. As if, before very long, there would be nothing left of the Alix Petrakos she knew. All she could do was vow not to give in without a fight, to make sure any victory Pierce achieved would be a hollow one.

CHAPTER SEVEN

THE wedding took place two days later. It was, by circumstance, a quiet affair, with only her mother and a friend of Pierce's in attendance. Alix wouldn't have had it any other way, because to her mind the fact that they were getting married at all made a mockery of what she had always believed to be a sacred institution. The only way she knew she would get through it at all was to think of her father.

The civil ceremony was short. Alix had chosen to wear an ivory silk suit and matching pillbox hat, complete with a pearl-dotted veil, on her head. She also, very reluctantly, carried a small posy of flowers which her mother had pressed on her when she arrived. Her main memory of the service was the surprising strength of Pierce's responses. He managed to make it sound as if the vows they exchanged meant something to him, which she knew couldn't possibly be true. Superstitiously, it sent a chill down her spine.

The photographer came as a surprise when, as husband and wife, they once more walked into the sunshine. She should have known Pierce wouldn't let the event go by unrecorded, but a cold lump lodged under her heart as it only seemed to add to the sham. Fortunately, there was to be no reception. It was an ideal arrangement as far as Alix was concerned, for she doubted if she could hide for very much longer that the bride and groom were barely on speaking terms. Since their last confrontation, the atmosphere between them had been chilly almost to the point of frostbite.

'I'll just have one of you kissing the bride,' the photographer directed, either not catching the atmosphere or choosing to ignore it.

Alix would have liked to refuse, but with her mother watching, and the small crowd of onlookers—which a wedding always seemed to draw—looking on, didn't dare. Obediently she turned her face up to her husband's.

'I feel like a performing seal!' she muttered tersely, as Pierce's hand steadied her chin.

'Maybe, but a very beautiful one,' he returned husklly.

Her breath caught at something that flickered momentarily in his eyes, but before she could analyse it his mouth was on hers and her lashes fluttered down helplessly. It was the strangest kiss she had ever received from him, and all the more staggering for that. No passion, or possession, but rather an amalgam of elation and relief, so that when he raised his head again she could only stare up at him in confusion. That clearly satisfied him, because Pierce merely smiled and released her.

'That's enough,' he declared, cutting off the photographer in mid-flow, and turned to his new mother-in-law. 'If we don't get going, we'll miss our flight. Take care of yourself, Emily, and tell Stephen not to worry while we're away. There's a good team in charge, so all he has to do is concentrate on getting well.'

Emily Petrakos made some sort of watery response as she kissed his cheek, then turned to her daughter and hugged her. 'You looked beautiful. Be happy, darling. Pierce is a good man. He'll take care of you all right.'

Such confidence, which once she had shared, brought a lump to her throat. However, it wasn't in Alix to disillusion her parent, so she quickly returned the hug to hide the despair that she feared must show in her eyes. 'I know he is, and I'll do my best.'

All that was left for them to do was climb into the waiting car and wave farewell as they began the journey to the airport. Biting her lip against a foolish wave of emotional tears, Alix sat back with a sigh, already feeling drained by the effort to act normally. Things weren't normal, and never could be. At least she didn't have to pretend with Pierce. He knew exactly what her feelings were. Her lips curved wryly as she surveyed the posy still clasped in her hand, then she tossed it aside into the gap she had been careful to leave between them.

To her surprise, she heard Pierce move, and when she glanced round she discovered that he had picked it up.

'The flowers aren't your enemy, Alix,' he reproved softly, smoothing back bruised petals. 'Although I imagine it's me you'd like to leave crushed.'

She would, but the truth was the reverse, for she was the one usually left wilted and defeated. 'You're unbreakable. A solid block of stone,' she responded tightly, watching in perplexity as he leaned over to place the posy on the front passenger seat, all the while speaking rapidly in Greek to the driver, who, she had discovered, travelled the world with him.

When he sat back, he eased sideways so that he could watch her more easily. 'Stone is breakable if you hit it in the right place.'

'You mean, if I keep looking, I'll find your weak spot?' she asked in mocking disbelief.

A smile tugged at the corner of his lips. 'It's patently obvious to those with eyes to see. Who knows? If you saw it, you might not want to break it at all.'

She frowned at that, somehow feeling that he was telling her something in a code she didn't know how to unscramble. Irritated that he could unsettle her so easily, she sat more upright. 'I guess I'm not that forgiving.' Her eyes fell on the back of the chauffeur's head. 'Why did you give him my flowers? What did you say?'

'I told him to take them and have them preserved. You might like to keep them in the bedroom as a reminder of today.'

Her eyes dropped to the chased gold band which now graced her marriage finger. It had been the source of another fruitless battle. She had wanted something simple, but Pierce had insisted, and, as usual, got his way. She had been surprised when the best man had produced two rings, a matching one for her to place on Pierce's finger too. She hadn't imagined he would want a permanent reminder of his wedded state.

'Are either of us likely to forget it? I know I won't need reminding,' she advised coolly.

'Nevertheless, it shall be done. Who knows? You may change your mind,' Pierce argued reasonably, picking up her left hand and studying the effect of the gold on her slim hand. 'My ring suits you. What did you do with the others?'

Her nerves jolted for two reasons: at that reminder of the other time, and the tingle of awareness his light touch sent shooting up her arm. She gasped, attempting to pull her hand free, but he denied her.

'Does my touch revolt you, Alix?' he taunted, the tone and curve of his lips telling her he knew otherwise.

Forced to sit still, she went on the defensive. 'Everything about you revolts me!' she lied desperately. 'As for your rings, I was tempted to throw them into the

Hudson River, but it seemed a waste of good money. So I gave them to the first charity I came across.'

'I'm glad to know they went to a worthy cause,' he responded, ironically.

Alix seethed impotently. 'Money is all you're good for!'

He laughed. 'Really? I'll remind you of that when you're writhing in my arms tonight.'

Colour stung her cheeks as she realised she had walked right into that. It was a subject she had been religiously avoiding thinking about, viewing the prospect with alarm. An alarm caused by the knowledge that, whatever her brain decreed, her body wanted him quite desperately. Each hour that passed made the fight harder to keep up. But he had just given her some much needed ammunition. 'You conceited... Will you *please* let me go?'

Pierce sent her a quizzical look. 'What's so wrong about a husband wanting to hold his wife's hand? Especially when they've just been married.'

Alix breathed in deeply, determined to remain cool. 'Don't be a hypocrite. There's no need for us to play games now, Pierce. There's nobody watching us who needs to be impressed,' she retorted scornfully.

Another small smile twitched the corners of his mouth. 'And what if I tell you I'm not playing games?'

Grey eyes flashed him an old-fashioned look. 'I wouldn't believe you.'

Sighing elaborately, Pierce crossed his legs but still kept a firm hold on her hand. 'However our marriage may have come about, I intend to do my best to make it work, Alix. You could do the same,' he suggested softly, and her heart kicked in her chest.

Lord, he sounded so plausible, but she knew from past experience just what an actor he was. 'There's no need to go to so much trouble on my account!' she shot back, and this time found her hand released when she tugged.

'Oh, it's no trouble, darling. It's what I always intended.'

His answer came as a complete surprise, and she stared at him in astonishment. 'You make it sound as if you wanted this marriage,' she said slowly, and received only a raised brow for her pains.

Unable to sustain that look, she turned away, staring out of the window, frowning heavily. Surely Pierce couldn't have wanted to marry her? That made no sense. She was an unwanted ex-wife. Except, of course, that he did want her. But you didn't have to marry someone to satisfy a sexual urge. He could have blackmailed her into an affair, but he hadn't. Had it had to be marriage or nothing? And just what did that mean?

Rather late in the day, it occurred to her to ask, and she turned to him once more. 'Just why did you marry me, Pierce? You could have helped my father without that. If you wanted the Petrakos empire, you could have bought your way in. Why on earth did you want to tie yourself to me again?' She was trying to put together the mental pieces of a puzzle which was getting harder instead of easier.

For a moment Pierce returned her look, then turned to gaze out of the window. 'I had my reasons, but you aren't ready to hear them yet,' he told her evenly, and that struck an all too familiar chord, rousing her sleeping temper.

'Oh, yes, I forgot, you like to pick your moment, don't you? You have a penchant for early morning, I recall. Should I get my armour ready for tomorrow?' she taunted, voice unconsciously registering a mixture of anger and pain.

He turned at that, eyes revealing a deep regret that he didn't even attempt to hide. 'Relax, Alix, this time there will be no surprises. You'll know the right time as well as I,' he declared softly.

Alix found her heart was beating faster. He was confusing her, just when she knew she needed to be thinking clearly. 'Why should I trust you?'

His smile was lop-sided. 'That's something I can't make you do. You either will or you won't.'

She bit her lip, for some unaccountable reason feeling anxious. 'I don't understand you.'

Pierce's smile became self-mocking. 'You never did,' he answered enigmatically, and she raised her chin.

'Well, if there had ever been a time I might have wanted to, I certainly don't now.' There were too many scars, too much pain, she thought, feeling choked by too much remembered emotion. Turning away, she fixed her attention on the outside world, distancing herself as best she could from the man beside her.

Yet her thoughts couldn't be so easily turned off. Pierce had to be playing a game. He was trying to undermine her; of that she was becoming increasingly certain. The first subtle signs had caught her attention only days ago, during one of the meetings he had had with various influential businessmen, many of whom she had seen recently herself. Recalling the chilly nature of their latest confrontation, she had assumed Pierce's insistence that she be present was to put her nose out of

joint, but the first few minutes showed her the error in
her thinking. It wasn't her nose he intended to disjoint,
but those of the men who had come to see him to curry
favour. They hadn't quite liked having to talk to Pierce
in her presence, but she had been honest enough to admit
that she enjoyed their discomfiture. And then she had
met Pierce's amused conspiratorial look, experiencing a
surge of warmth inside her, because, incredible as it
might seem, that look had suggested that he had engin-
eered the whole confrontation for her.

Yet she couldn't imagine why he should have, and of
course she hadn't been able to ask him. She had thought
it one of those rare moments of empathy which even the
worst enemies could have. Yet now her feminine instinct
told her it was more than that, only she couldn't fully
define why. All she knew for certain was that she had
to be on the alert, because . . . Because she sensed danger
ahead—a sensation so strong that it had been waking
her in the night, to find her heart beating as fast as if
she had been running for her life. Even now, in the light
of day, it remained her overriding memory.

The island stretched out ahead, appearing to drift lazily
in the sparkling blue sea. Alix had been watching it since
it was a mere pin-point on the horizon. Pierce had been
deliberately mysterious, only admitting that they were
going to stay at a villa he had on a Greek island when
she had recognised Athens earlier in the day. There, they
had transferred from his private jet to a helicopter which
had brought them the rest of the way.

Now she gazed down on their ultimate destination. It
looked idyllic, far greener than she would have expected. At any other time she would have been looking

forward to spending time there, but her heart sank at the thought of being locked up with him in such splendid isolation. Although she hated them as a rule, she would have given anything to be heading for some crowded cosmopolitan resort, instead of this tiny corner of paradise.

Feeling Pierce's eyes on her, she glanced round, trying not to react to the sight of him. Earlier he had removed his jacket and tie, loosed the buttons of his shirt to reveal a tantalising glimpse of his throat and rolled up his sleeves. He looked as relaxed as he could in the circumstances, and her senses had rocked accordingly. For pure unconscious sensuality he had no peer, his maleness arousing her femininity without any effort at all. It was impossible to be unaware of him, and she was finding it increasingly difficult to pretend indifference—a fact she was pretty sure he was all too aware of.

Now she found the lazy warmth of his gaze disconcerting. Somewhere over Europe there had been a subtle change in him, a relaxation of the tension she was used to sensing in him, plus something more, which she might have called contentment, had it been any other man. The result was shattering to senses so finely tuned to him, as if he was sending out subliminal messages which her body understood even if she didn't, and she dropped her eyes, glad that she had an excuse to do so. 'Is this the only way to get to the island?' she asked, although she had to clear her throat to get the words out.

'No, but it's the quickest. Why, are you looking for an escape route already?' he queried sardonically.

His teasing, another sign of that strange mood he had fallen into, made her feel hotter than she was already. Her hat had disappeared a long time ago, but she hadn't been able to remove her jacket because she only wore a camisole underneath it, and she was damned if she would give him a free show. So she had suffered in silence, tormented by the lure of the sea that she longed to fling her overheated body into.

'Will I need one?' she countered tiredly, and felt rather than saw him shrug.

'Who knows with you? But there are no shortage of them. The islanders run a successful fishing fleet, any one of which would take you across to the mainland if you asked them. This is not a prison, Alix,' he finished quietly, and once more she felt that wave of confusion rise up around her——

Until she remembered that the vows she had taken today were a prison of themselves. Of course he wasn't worried that she would try to escape the island, for he knew it was her own sense of honour which would keep her at his side. He had bought her, hadn't he? She had sold herself, and he was entitled to think he would get his money's worth, she thought bitterly.

Just why a fact which she had always known should make her feel so depressed she didn't understand. She had been all right until she had seen the island. Why should the sight of it suddenly make her want things she knew she couldn't expect to have? And just what did she want anyway? She didn't know that either. Everything was as it should be, and yet it wasn't. The parameters had changed in a subtle way that seemed to be undermining her. She had never felt so hunted and so ... scared.

That was enough to rally her spirit, and she told herself not to be such a fanciful idiot. Far better to concentrate on their arrival. The helicopter circled the island, giving her a spectacular view of the busy harbour, before making for the southern tip, where a low rambling white building with a terracotta-coloured roof sat basking in the late afternoon sunshine. They landed on an open area of ground behind the house, and as Pierce helped her to alight two men appeared through the surrounding trees. They greeted him like old friends, and from their wide smiles and voluble welcomes it was obvious that they already knew he was here with his new bride.

Alix stood back, feeling like an outsider. Her grandfather had cut his ties with his country many years ago, so there had been no insistence on his children, or their children, speaking Greek. It occurred to her that if they were going to spend any amount of time here she would have to learn quickly. When Pierce introduced them to her as Costas and Spiro, who took care of the property, she accepted their good wishes with a warm smile.

Pierce took her arm and led her towards the house while the two men dealt with their luggage. 'Would you like to see over the house now, or clean up first?' he asked as they stepped into the shadowed coolness of the building.

Alix felt as if she would scream if she didn't get out of her suit soon. 'Later. I'd like to wash and put on something cooler,' she admitted with a wry smile.

Blue eyes ran lightly over her, yet still had the power to raise the hairs on her skin. 'You do look a little wilted,' he agreed drily. 'The main bedroom's this way.'

The room he led her to was large and airy, decorated in shades of peach. The bathroom and dressing-rooms were off to one side, while a sliding glass door offered a breathtaking view out to sea. Yet it was the king-size bed which dominated the room. In Alix's mind it assumed giant proportions, causing a shiver to chase its way along her spine—a reaction which was only partly due to anxiety.

Pierce easily followed her gaze. 'Why don't you take a nap, Alix? It's been a hectic day. You take the shower here; I'll use the one next door this time. There's no rush; we don't eat until late.'

It wasn't dinner which worried her as she watched him walk into one of the dressing-rooms, emerging only seconds later with a change of clothing. It was the subtle manoeuvre which declared that this was his room, too, but he was prepared to give her space—for now. Later, however, was a different matter.

With his departure, Alix let out a ragged breath. She kicked off her shoes and thankfully stripped away the damply clinging suit. As she padded through to the bathroom, the sunken bath drew her gaze. It had a jacuzzi, too, and she instantly abandoned the idea of a shower for a long refreshing soak in the bubbling water.

It didn't take long for the tension to seep out of her, and she relaxed against the side, closing her eyes. Thoughts came then, unwelcome ones which could no longer be held back. There had been too much to think of earlier to worry about the night ahead, but here, with the bedroom only yards away, it came sharply into focus. Her lips tightened in a bitter line. Once there had been a time when she had longed for the night, wanting only to be with Pierce, but this was different. This time she was in his debt. He had bought the right to sleep with her.

A moan forced its way from her tight throat, as what felt like a stake was being driven through her heart. Lord, how she hated the thought of that. To be reduced to paying a debt! It diminished her and all that she felt. And that thought stopped her heart for vital seconds before it began again with a lurch. What on earth did she mean, all that she felt? She felt nothing! Nothing except hatred for the man who had so cruelly used and deceived her. Yet with another groan she knew she lied, and raised a hand to cover her eyes.

Honesty forced itself into her consciousness, and, once there, clung on tenaciously, making her at last admit the truth to herself. The reason she so hated the idea of paying a debt was because she wanted the marriage to be real. Above all, she wanted Pierce's love... because she loved him. Which had to make her the worst kind of fool alive!

Despair choked her even as she had an almost irresistible urge to laugh. Like Pandora, she had opened her box, and there was nothing she could do but face what came out. At last she admitted the final act of self-betrayal. Even in those first painful days of loss five years ago, in her heart she had crazily hoped that Pierce would one day come along and admit it had all been a mistake, that he did love her after all!

All this because she loved him. Had loved him, did love him—would always love him.

But she couldn't *still* love him! Not after all he had done—was still doing. He had used her, was still using her. How could she still love a man who could do that?

She didn't know, she only knew that she did—irrevocably. And if he ever found out, what might he not do? The power that would give him would be total. She could not give him that victory. Now, more than ever, she must continue to fight him, for it was the only way to conquer herself. Pierce must never find out the strength of her weakness. She might be committed to him, might have to sleep with him, but he must never have dominion over her heart and soul as he had before. She would take her secret to the grave.

'Don't fall asleep, Alix. I wouldn't want to lose you so soon,' a husky male voice drawled near her ear, and her eyes shot open.

Pierce hunkered down beside her, and it was a measure of just how lost she had been in her thoughts that her antennae hadn't picked up his entrance. Alarmed and angry in equal measure, Alix sat up, only to realise that she was revealing far too much of herself, and immediately sank down beneath the water again. But not before his eyes had taken their fill, and a lazy smile tugged at his lips.

'Surely you're not shy, darling? After all, you haven't got anything I haven't seen before.'

The mocking comment brought a flush of colour to her cheeks. 'I don't happen to be in the habit of giving men a free peep-show!' she spluttered back, feeling more at a disadvantage than she ever had before, not just from her nakedness, but from the revelations which had shaken her only moments before. 'You said you'd use the other bathroom,' she reminded him pungently.

One eyebrow quirked. 'I did, almost an hour ago,' he confirmed, drawing her gaze to the casual trousers and shirt he now wore. 'It occurred to me you might be avoiding me, so I came looking for you.'

Alix drew in a ragged breath. 'Well, you found me. Now I'd like to have some privacy.'

Blue eyes narrowed at her tone. 'Don't order me about, Alix. I'm your husband, not a servant, and I've every right to be here.'

She easily could have saved the situation with a few words, but they were beyond her. Because she was unsettled already, his declaration merely made her feel more threatened, and instinct had her defences rising.

'Oh, your rights! Now I understand. It's time to collect, isn't it?' she charged, sitting up once more, holding herself proudly. 'Never let it be said I reneged. Where do you want to do it? Here? I'm told it can be quite fun, if you don't mind drowning. Of course, there's the floor, or if you're more conventional we can go into the bedroom.'

So intent was she in self-protection that she quite failed to see the anger forming on her husband's face. He looked ready to explode, and when she came to a halt he thrust himself to his full height.

'That's enough! How dare you make yourself out to be some sort of whore?'

Alix quailed a little then, as she looked up at him, but there was no going back. 'Isn't that what they call it when a man buys a woman? I was bought, and now I'm fully prepared to pay the debt. I'm yours to command, aren't I?'

She had wanted to get through his icy control, and she did, but in a way she had never expected. Wide-eyed, she watched the smouldering anger in him ignite, and gasped as, careless of his clothes, he stepped down into the water and yanked her to her feet. With a cry of alarm, she was swept into his arms as he waded out again and strode towards the bedroom.

'You've gone too damn far this time, Alix,' he growled, and, ignoring the water streaming from them both, tossed her down on top of the bed. 'If you want to pay, then damn it, you can!'

Before she could say a word, Pierce threw himself down on top of her, grinding his mouth down on hers with a ferocity that drew blood. Alix whimpered. It was too late now to wish she hadn't pushed him so far. All she had wanted to do was protect herself, to prove to him she didn't care, but she had roused the sleeping tiger, and didn't now dare let go. He plundered her mouth until she was breathless. There was nothing of the Pierce she knew in the caresses of the man who quelled her struggles with crushing ease. His touch on her breasts, her belly and thighs, was insulting in its indifference. It was the very greediness she had accused him of, but which she knew was alien to his nature. Tears squeezed out of her eyes, because she had driven him to this, and had only herself to blame for the consequences. She felt unclean, like a woman bought solely for a man's pleasure, with no thought given to hers.

She knew that if he didn't stop she didn't have the strength to prevent him taking her in anger. Yet even as that destructive thought came Pierce uttered a strangled cry and thrust himself away from her. The same move carried him to his feet, where for one harrowing moment he stood and stared down at her, breathing fast. He seemed to be fighting demons of his own, then without a word he turned on his heel and left the room, crashing the door behind him.

Alix remained spread-eagled on the bed as first one sob and then another tore through her. She raised her hands to her eyes, but the tears refused to be held back, and she rolled over, burying her head in the pillows. She cried until there were nothing more than hiccups left, feeling drained...and ashamed. What had happened had been her fault. She had over-reacted, and had been lucky not to suffer more than acute self-disgust. What had happened to her cool sophistication? It had vanished with the knowledge that she could never be indifferent to Pierce. She had been so afraid of giving him the power to hurt her again. Instead, she had invited him to hurt her in a different way.

Climbing wearily to her feet, she shuddered as she saw the ruined state of the bed. Dragging off the wet sheets, she carried them into the bathroom, shoving them into the laundry basket. Then her eye caught the still bubbling bath, and, feeling nauseous, she shut it off and drained it. Only then did she step into the shower and scrub herself free of the taint of her own folly. Later she dried herself on a huge fluffy towel before wrapping herself in a towelling robe she noticed hanging behind the door.

Back in the bedroom, she discovered not only that a tray of tea had miraculously appeared, but that her cases had been unpacked, and the bed remade. It was uncomfortable to imagine what that unknown person must have thought about the latter—probably that she and Pierce had been overcome by passion, and hadn't cared about their wet state before tumbling into bed. It brought colour to her cheeks, and she badly needed the cup of tea she poured for herself.

Calmer now, she found it easier to think. She had been a fool, and now she knew she had to try and salvage something out of the mess, or their marriage would be untenable. Her pride had almost caused the worst fall of all, and it was up to her to apologise. Where they went from there who could tell...? Only the gods.

* * *

It was growing dark quickly now. Alix knew it was a pointless exercise to glance at her watch; it would only tell her that another ten minutes had passed, adding to the hours since Pierce had left her.

She was sitting on the terrace, where Katina, Spiro's wife, had brought her coffee an hour ago. Nothing had been said about the missing bridegroom, nor about the fact that the bride had dined alone, merely picking at the splendidly prepared meal. The silence had been eloquent to Alix, making her wish she hadn't dressed with such care, or applied her make-up to conceal the ravages of her tears. All for a man who hadn't appeared.

She chewed at her lip. Anger had long ago given way to worry. Where was he? What was he doing? Had he hurt himself? Was he lying somewhere, badly injured, praying for help? It was no use telling herself not to be silly, that he knew the island very well. Each passing minute it grew darker, and with it grew her anxiety.

Even as she remonstrated with herself, suddenly the hairs seemed to stand up all over her skin, and her head turned. Still in the shadows, Pierce stood watching her. He had come upon her quietly, like before, but this time her main emotion was relief. She knew that, had anything happened to him, she would never have forgiven herself. He moved, coming into the light so that she had an excellent view of the grim set of his face. His eyes were hooded, giving nothing away. Alix found she was holding her breath, knowing she had to speak before her courage failed her.

She licked dry lips nervously. 'Pierce, I——'

'No!' The sharpness of that one word cut her off. 'No, my sweet wife, you had your say earlier; now it's my turn,' Pierce declared shortly. 'I'm not about to apologise for what happened, Alix. I know you'd rather I'd carried on, taken you against your will. That way you could continue to hate me, couldn't you? Unfortunately, I'm not going to play your game. It isn't going to be like that. My rules, Alix. You come to me. I want you, but I'm a patient man. I'll wait until you come to me, and you will come, because you're a passionate, sensual woman. When the time comes, you'll have to ask me, because there will be no repetition of today.' Now he leaned towards her, bringing his lancing gaze dangerously close. 'I won't lay a finger on you until you beg me to, understand?'

Alix felt her throat close over, and a shiver chased its way down her spine. It didn't help to know that she had brought this situation on herself. All thought of apologising was gone with the wind. Her chin came up as she prepared to do battle. 'You'll have a long wait.'

He laughed tonelessly. 'I'm prepared for that—but I don't think it will be as long as you imagine,' he amended, and after one more all-encompassing look walked away into the villa.

Alix caught her breath as that last statement hit home. How dared he suggest she'd come running after him? He wasn't as irresistible as he imagined! But wasn't he? a small voice jeered at her, and she winced. Well, maybe he was, but she had done without him all these years, and she could keep on the same way. For one thing was certain—she would never beg him, never. There would be no truce between them now, just a battle she couldn't afford to lose.

CHAPTER EIGHT

ALIX listened to the sound of the shower running in the bathroom with a heavy heart. Her head turned, allowing her to see the indentation in the next pillow where Pierce's head had rested last night. The fact of his presence in the bed had produced their first skirmish, and she had lost it. When she had walked into the bedroom the evening before, Pierce had already been in the bed. She had come to an abrupt halt when she had seen him propped up against the headboard, bare to the waist, and, if she knew anything about him, bare to his toes too. He had been reading, but he had looked up at her entry.

'Let me know if the light bothers you,' he had advised coolly, as if their sharing a bed were an everyday occurrence, and Alix had bristled.

'As I have no intention of sharing so much as a room with you, let alone a bed, it hardly matters,' she had snapped, disgusted with herself for having to tear her eyes away from the wide expanse of tanned male flesh on view. Damn him, she knew he had done it on purpose!

'On the contrary, darling, you won't be sleeping anywhere else,' he had countered mildly, albeit with a steely glint in his eye.

Whereupon she had crossed her arms in a belligerent pose. Nothing on this earth would get her to agree. 'You can hardly stop me simply turning and walking out.'

His teeth had flashed as he grinned. 'True, but that will only make me have to come and get you—something I'm prepared to do, however many times it takes. This is our bed, and here you sleep.'

Alix had stared at him in impotent fury, knowing he would be as good as his word. He'd carry her kicking and screaming if he had to.

'What's the matter, Alix? Are you afraid to sleep with me? Are you afraid you won't be able to keep your hands off me?' he had taunted next, and she had risen instantly to the bait, as he had known she would.

She hadn't said a word, just collected her nightdress and gone to change in the bathroom. The ultimate indignity had been to find that he had turned out the light and already had his back to her when she returned. He hadn't doubted for a minute that she would do as she was told! Of course, it had been impossible to sleep, especially when she could hear Pierce's rhythmic breathing, telling her that he had had no such problem. She had tossed and turned for hours, only falling asleep as the sky had begun to lighten.

Now she stared at his pillow, and something stronger than her will-power had her rolling over, pressing her head into the hollow, breathing in the lingering scent of him. A soft groan left her lips. Last night had been a refinement of torture. She had been excruciatingly aware of him, made worse by the knowledge that all she had had to do was reach across the space dividing them and touch him, and he would have turned to her, accepting her surrender to the inevitable. She had been sorely tempted, and knew that it would only get worse, not better.

With another groan, this time of self-disgust at her maudlin behaviour, she sat up. How on earth could she even consider giving in? She had her pride, didn't she? But that was cold comfort, as she had known for a long time. Pride didn't hold you close during the long hours of night, or bring the most indescribable, yet exquisite pleasure of loving.

The shower stopped, and she tensed instantly. Not wishing to be caught still in bed, Alix reached for her silk robe which lay on the ottoman at the foot of the bed, and froze. For on it rested one perfect pink rosebud. Her heart contracted, then raced madly as she tentatively picked it up. The scent was heady, sending all manner of wild thoughts through her mind. Where had it come from ... and why was it here, on her robe?

'A rose for a rose.'

The unexpected sound of Pierce's voice caused Alix to jump violently, jabbing her thumb on a thorn. She winced as her head jerked round, as much startled by his noiseless approach as the husky note of sincerity in his voice. As she doubted her hearing, he came towards her, a towel slung low about his hips, the slicked-back blue-black hair gleaming wetly. Before she could stop him, he had taken hold of her hand, examining the small welling of blood.

'It was supposed to please you, not hurt you,' he declared gruffly, and raised her hand to his lips, licking the blood away.

Alix's senses swam dizzily for a moment or two, swamped by the caring tone and the sensual caress of his tongue. This was not the man she had come to know, to her cost. He was more like the lover she had known in the beginning, five years ago. Since then, she had learned that he did nothing without a reason. That cleared her mind wonderfully. Her suspicion sharpened. What was he up to now?

With a sharp intake of breath, she pulled her hand away from that tantalising touch. 'Roses, Pierce?' she queried sardonically. 'What did I do to deserve this ... token of your esteem?' She managed to instil a healthy dose of scorn into the words, acknowledging as she did so that they were as much for her benefit as his—a reminder that she must not fall into the same trap as before.

Her husband didn't rise to her bait. 'Nothing. Perhaps I decided to lay my heart at your feet for you to walk over this time.'

Her lips parted on a silent gasp. He couldn't really be saying he cared for her, could he? That he was offering her her revenge? The answer came back violently; no. Not Pierce Martineau. He was just toying with her again, probing for a way through to her. And she knew only one reason for that—to undermine her resolve to resist him. Her face pinched up, and she crossed swiftly to the waste basket, tossing the flower into it. Yet not without a twinge of compunction for the damage to such a perfect bloom. Whenever she and Pierce came together, something beautiful was destroyed.

She turned her back on it, raising her chin to him. 'In order to do that, you'd first have to have a heart.' Pierce's chest expanded magnificently as he took a deep breath, and it wasn't lost on her, though she pretended otherwise. The last thing she needed was to be side-tracked.

'You think I don't have one?' Pierce asked as he moved to the patio doors, leaning back against the frame so that the sunlight set off the play of muscles under his skin.

Alix was drawn to the sight as if by a magnet; it should have pleased but didn't. 'I know you don't. I have a very good memory.' There had been another morning, the only one when she had faced him like this, and he had taunted her with the reason he had married her. Pain darkened her eyes, and Pierce's eyes narrowed on her, before he, too, tensed.

'Nothing like that is going to happen this time, Alix,' he promised her in that same husky tone, and her nerves skittered in violent reaction.

'I wouldn't let it. I'll never be foolish enough to make myself that vulnerable to you ever again, Pierce,' she declared, with a bravado only she was aware of. Because she was vulnerable, terrifyingly so.

Pierce eyed her broodingly. 'We have to talk about the past some time.'

A proposition which had her shaking her head. 'There's nothing to say. I was there. I know all I need to know.'

His mouth curved wryly. 'And perhaps you saw only what I wanted you to see. Did that ever occur to you, Alix?' he queried, pushing himself upright and moving a step or two closer, causing her to breathe in sharply.

'When someone has used a steamroller on you, you don't look to see if they've stabbed you too! The result was the same. You committed murder. If you're suddenly looking for absolution, Pierce, go to a priest, don't come to me!' Alix railed at him from the midst of her never-to-be-forgotten pain.

She knew she had scored a hit when his face closed up. 'Absolution? Perhaps that is what I want, but not from you. I discovered it's easier to forgive others than to forgive yourself.'

Alix laughed, but it was a painful effort from a tight throat. 'Could this really be compunction from the mighty Pierce Martineau? Are you trying to convince me you regret what you did?'

There was a brief jerk of a muscle in his jaw. 'Is it not allowed?'

She stared into eyes that suddenly seemed clouded by something she didn't understand. It might have been sadness, and she might even have softened but for the fact of remembering just how good an actor he was. 'I'll tell you what it is, it's unbelievable! You're just as hard and conniving as you ever were, Pierce, and you'll never get me to think otherwise.'

His eyes cleared miraculously, and were refilled by a mixture of irritation and mockery, upholding her view that what she had seen hadn't been real. 'If that was so, why did you spend the night curled up in my arms?' he challenged, taking her breath away.

'I never did!' she spluttered. 'I was on my own side of the bed when I woke.'

One eyebrow drifted skywards. 'Only because I put you there. Only because you finally allowed me to. When I tried to do the same in the small hours, you refused to let me go. You were as soft as a kitten but as clinging as a vine. Although I was tempted to wake you up and investigate the turn of events, I thought you'd rather wake up on your own.'

Oh, God, why did the statement have the ring of truth about it? Aghast, hot colour flooded her cheeks. 'You're lying!'

'Not about this. It seems your subconscious knows where you want to be; it's only your stubborn pride that's stopping you admitting it openly.'

Forced to accept the truth, she writhed inwardly. 'So that you can gloat about your victory?'

Pierce emitted a long-suffering sigh. 'I seem to remember telling you this time it would be different. You don't have much faith, darling.'

'You cured me of my naïveté a long time ago. Do you wonder that my faith in your word was shattered too? Like Humpty Dumpty, there are some things you can never put back together again.' The words left her lips with their bitterness intact. She might still love him, but she doubted if she would ever fully trust him again.

Pierce remained quite still for a moment as they stared at each other, then he reached out to trace one finger down the curve of her cheek. 'We reap only what we sow,' he murmured obliquely, then shrugged and moved towards his dressing-room. 'Get dressed, Alix. I've arranged for us to take the yacht out after breakfast.'

The command irritated her, so much so that she responded childishly, 'Perhaps I don't want to go on a yacht.'

Halfway through the door, he turned to her with a mocking smile. 'You once told me you loved sailing. Do you intend to cut off your nose to spite your face?'

He had her over a barrel, but the thought of sticking to her guns, and so missing out on sailing those crystal-clear waters, was too depressing. 'No,' she admitted reluctantly, and his smile softened.

'Then wear something protective. The sun can be hot here, and I wouldn't want you to get ill on the first day of our honeymoon,' he cautioned as he disappeared.

Alix was left with the uncomfortable feeling that she had been outmanoeuvred in more ways than one. Pierce had changed tack overnight, and she would have to be very much on her guard. Yet even that could not dampen her enthusiasm for the proposed outing, and it was with a strangely light heart that she went to shower and dress.

It was the sort of day that lingered in the memory. Pierce, in cut-off denim shorts and nothing else, steered the amazingly modest vessel out to sea, with Alix, in fashionable twill shorts and baggy cotton top over a royal blue swimsuit, a willing deckhand. It was impossible to sail a boat and remain in a bad mood, and before long they were both relaxed and laughing. It could have been the warmth of the sun, or the sound of water beneath the bows, or just the glorious feeling of the breeze whipping through her hair, but Alix suddenly realised that, for the first time for as long as she could remember, she was happy.

Her guard dropped.

With the sails set, Alix had the opportunity to sit back and watch Pierce as he stood at the helm, long straight legs braced, the fluid lines of his body rippling and flexing as he made the minute adjustments to keep them on the course he had chosen. He looked at one with the environment, more at home in scruffy shorts than handmade suits. It was impossible not to look at him and feel her heart swell. There was no adequate word to describe his kind of male perfection; she only knew he was beautiful to her eyes.

It brought a wistful expression to her eyes, a longing for things to be different, yet knowing they never could be. Then, because it was too beautiful a day for such maudlin thoughts, she shrugged them off, and when, only moments later, Pierce turned to smile at her, she could only smile back.

'Want a go?' he asked, indicating the wheel, and she didn't hesitate to take the challenge.

It was a heady sensation of power to feel the boat responding to her smallest command, but nothing like the shivering heat of response to Pierce's body as he stood behind her. For once they were at peace, at one with each other, and she threw back her head with a laugh of pure joy.

'I take it you're glad you came?' Pierce commented, and she could hear the smile in his voice.

Alix tipped her head back, eyes sparkling up at him. 'I hadn't realised how much I'd missed this,' she admitted. There had been little time for such pastimes lately.

Blue eyes softened as they roamed her features, then he dropped a swift kiss on her lips. 'Hmm, I thought it would please you,' he agreed, before reaching out to steady the wheel which had slipped through her fingers. 'Watch your course.'

Heart thumping, Alix forced herself to concentrate on what she was doing, but it proved difficult. That brief kiss had shot through her system like a powerful jolt of electricity. But it was his words which brought the faint frown to her brow.

'Is that why we're here, to please me?' she queried huskily.

'Can you think of a better idea?' he countered smoothly.

Alix responded with a shiver to the warmth of his tone. 'To please you,' she offered, unable to raise the defences that a small voice of caution was advising her to do.

'Pleasing you pleases me, Alix,' Pierce replied easily, bringing his head down beside hers, using his arm to point ahead of them. 'Do you see that island? I thought we'd anchor there for lunch. We can swim too. Sound good?'

Alix had the crazy feeling that she didn't know if she was on her head or her heels. 'Very,' she admitted edgily, then simply had to ask, 'Pierce, why are you doing this? Why are you being so nice to me all of a sudden?'

'Don't you think you deserve being nice to?' he returned casually.

'It's not what I expect from you. There has to be some ulterior motive.'

'There is.'

That admittance turned her heart to ice, seeming to confirm everything she had already decided. 'So that you can get me into your bed without a fight,' she declared, tasting the bitterness of gall on her tongue.

'I could have done that any time, and you know it,' came the even reply.

It was a truth she didn't bother to deny. He possessed an irresistible magic for her that she could never conquer—and in all honesty didn't want to. But where did that leave her now? 'Then what is it you want?'

Pierce looked down at her then, his blue eyes revealing a surprising depth of self-mockery. 'A miracle, and there aren't too many of them around these days. What do you think the chances are?'

Alix caught her breath. He seemed to be probing her, searching for his answer deep in her soul. He almost seemed unsure, hesitant, and because that was so unlike him her reply sounded shaken. 'Slim.'

He laughed at that. 'You and I are tending to agree on more and more things every day. Here, you'd better let me take her in. Why don't you go down into the cabin and see what Katina has prepared for us?'

She did as he suggested only because she needed time to think. This morning she had thought she knew what he was after; now she wasn't so sure. A miracle, he had said, but he hadn't specified what kind. It implied there was something he wanted but wasn't sure he could have, and for Pierce that was unbelievable. She knew from experience that when he wanted something he went all out until he got it. Hadn't he used her to get the shipping line, and hadn't he used her loyalty and love for her father to get her as his wife again?

This uncertainty just didn't make sense, any more than the change in him since the moment they were married. There had been times when he had been almost lover-like. Things done to please her, to make her happy, as if he wanted the marriage to be a real one, and not the contract it surely was. Why did she feel as if she was hovering on the brink of making a fantastic discovery?

'Are you OK down there?' Pierce's disembodied voice interrupted her, and her head shot up as she belatedly realised they were now stationary.

'Just coming!' she called out, hastily looking for the food, and finding a coolbox tucked away under the table. Grabbing it, she was about to go up on deck when a pair of long legs appeared on the stairs and Pierce reached down to take the box from her. Their fingers touched briefly, and her eyes flew to his, to meet and flounder in the warmth they found there.

'Feels as if she's packed enough food for a siege. Do you want to eat now, or have a swim first?'

Alix gave up the struggle to fight through the confusion caused by his actions. Besides, she knew deep inside that she really didn't want to have to think at all. It might be the height of foolishness, but today she was simply going to take one step at a time.

So she sent him a grin. 'I've been longing for a swim,' she admitted, and Pierce laughed.

'I remember you were the original water baby. It was hard to get you out of the sea once you were in it,' he responded, eyes dancing.

She gave a gasp of outrage. 'I like that! You were just as bad, worse even. It's a wonder you ever got any work done!'

Pierce finished stripping off his shorts to reveal ultra-brief trunks, and sent her a mocking look. 'You didn't try to force me very hard. In fact, you were more of a distraction than the water.'

That wiped the smile from her face, leaving it haunted. 'Oh, I doubt that, although you did a good job of pretending,' she returned tightly, and turned her back on him to strip off her shorts and top.

'My passion for you was very real, Alix. That's one thing a man can't fake,' Pierce answered after a pause, and she swung round, lips curved ironically.

'But that was all. Anyway, it's in the past now.' Yet not forgotten. 'I'll race you to the beach,' she challenged, jumping up on the side and diving cleanly into the sparkling water.

There was no contest, but she had known that when she made the challenge. It had been done solely to divert them from too painful a topic. Pierce had always been the better swimmer, but he surprised her by keeping pace with her and not forging ahead as she had imagined he would. They reached the beach together, staggering into the shallows to collapse on to the wet sand, letting the gentle waves caress their legs.

'It was further than I thought,' she gasped, when she had enough breath to speak. 'I'm out of condition.'

Beside her, Pierce rolled on to his front. 'I wouldn't say that. You look in pretty good condition from here,' he replied teasingly, a remark which brought her head round swiftly.

Catching his eyes warmly caressing her feminine curves brought a deeper pink to her cheeks. She could feel her body respond as it always had, and because they were alone, and the temptation was to lower her defences, she instinctively raised them. 'There's no need to flirt with me.'

He eyed her broodingly. 'I know, but I enjoy it.'

She stifled a groan. 'Well, I don't.'

Pierce reached out to smooth a strand of hair from her cheek. 'You never used to be such a liar.'

It wasn't fair that even the briefest of touches could arouse her. 'We can't say the same about you, can we?' she shot back, expecting to see him close up, but instead he merely nodded.

'I amazed myself with just how good I was at it. But you know what they say—for the sins you do by two and two, you must pay for one by one.'

There was a quality to his voice which made her frown. 'Are you paying?'

Pierce sighed and rested his chin in his hand. 'I've been paying since the first lie left my lips. A fact which should please you, Alix. Don't you want to see me hurting?'

It was a direct question, and her heart answered without equivocation. No, she didn't want to see him hurting. After all these years she suddenly realised she had no taste for revenge. You couldn't love someone and want to hurt them, no matter what you might say or think in the heat of the moment.

Yet she couldn't openly admit it to him, for that would only make her more vulnerable. It was easier to raise her arm to cover her eyes and say evenly, 'I don't enjoy seeing anyone hurting. There's too much pain in the world as it is.'

'Thank you,' he said huskily, and she had to look at him then.

'For what?'

A wry smile twisted his lips. 'For including me. You always were a generous and loving woman. I'm glad to see the generosity hasn't faded. What about the loving?'

There was no way she could just lie there and answer that, and she sat up abruptly, knowing her face would be far too revealing. 'If you're trying to find out how many lovers I've had, then mind your own damned business,' she retorted, choosing to deliberately misunderstand.

'You haven't had any,' Pierce told her quietly, and her heart missed a beat before careering crazily on.

He sat up and she stared at him, aghast. 'W-what?' How on earth could he have known that? The answer struck her almost immediately. 'Do you mean to tell me you've had me followed?' she charged wrathfully, fingers curling into the sand.

'I prefer to call it keeping a friendly eye on you.'

Alix fumed impotently. 'You were never my friend, Pierce, and how dare you spy on me?'

'How else could I know you were in trouble and needed my help?' he informed her mildly. 'And when it comes to friendship, surely that's rated on the willingness of those to help you when you really need it. On that scale, I'm the best friend you've got.'

Though it hurt to admit it, put like that, he was absolutely right, and yet... 'You weren't helping me, you were helping yourself to my father's company!'

'I neither want, nor need the company. As it is, my financial advisers think I was a fool to take it on, because it's going to swallow money like a bottomless pit. Had it been anyone else I would have let it go to the wall,' Pierce told her without bothering to pull his punches, and Alix felt her chin drop.

She raised a hand to her temple, staring at him in disbelief. 'Are you saying you only saved the company because of me?'

'Nothing else would have tempted me to touch it with a barge pole,' he confessed drily, watching the emotions flounder across her face.

'But... why?'

One eyebrow lifted. 'Why? Have you ever read Lovelace?'

Her frown deepened. 'The poet? No.' Why on earth was he talking in riddles?

'Then perhaps you should,' was his only answer as he stood up and reached down a hand to her. Alix took it automatically, her eyes searching his as she stood before him. But Pierce's only showed an enigmatic smile. 'Let's go back. I'm hungry, and you're starting to go pink. You need to cover up or you'll burn.'

As he still had hold of her hand, and was already wading back into the water, there was little Alix could do but follow him, although her mind was teeming with questions. Once again Pierce kept pace with her as they swam back to the yacht, climbing aboard first to help her up. Yet even there he forestalled her intention to question him by throwing her a towel and turning his attention to the coolbox.

In no time at all he had laid out quite an array of food on the banquette seating between them, as well as opened a bottle of wine. The sight of food made her realise just how hungry she was, and for the moment she abandoned all thought of following up his amazing statement.

Neither of them spoke very much as they helped themselves to the various salads and cold meats. Alix relaxed again, and when she unfortunately bit into a tomato and sent the seeds dripping down her chin she couldn't help laughing.

'It's good to see you without a frown,' Pierce observed, laughing himself as he squatted in front of her, holding her chin as he mopped up the mess with a napkin.

Her laughter died. 'There hasn't been a lot to smile about,' she replied, more shortly than she intended, because she was very much aware of his touch.

Pierce went still. 'I know the feeling.'

Once again her eyes searched his, meeting a look which could only have been regret. She was at a loss to understand him, and sent him a sceptical glance. 'You do? I thought you would have been laughing all the way to the bank! I mean, the shipping line you stole from my grandfather—so it cost you nothing, but it's made you a fortune since!'

That strange expression vanished as the shutters came down, and he regarded her steadily. 'Strange how everything always comes back to this. You know the truth, Alix, although you refuse to accept it.'

Her eyes became stormy. 'It was his pride and joy!'

Anger flashed in his eyes too. 'Then why did he let it rot? It was a symbol, Alix, a constant reminder of how he had outwitted my grandfather, his most hated enemy. In repair it could have earned him a fortune, but he chose to see it rot rather than sell it. I took nothing that didn't rightfully belong to me.'

About to deny it vehemently, she paused, because what he said had a ring of truth. She had always assumed that her grandfather had loved the fleet of ships, but if he had why had they been rotting away? Not for want of money, for to Yannis Petrakos the cost of repairs would have been a mere drop in the ocean. It smacked more of vengeful spite. Of the hatred Pierce insisted had ruled his actions. And hadn't she always known that her grandfather was a hard man? Generous so long as you did what he wanted and knew your place. Her father had not been willing to accept it, and had left to form his own life—a life which had included no bitterness towards the Andreas family.

Pierce, who had watched the play of emotions across her face as her silence lengthened, gave her a tiny shake. 'Now do you understand?'

She did, but there was so much more than that. 'What if I do? It excuses nothing. The end can never justify the means. It doesn't excuse the way you used me to get the ships back for nothing!' she countered shakily.

Releasing her, Pierce stood up, expression mocking. 'On the contrary, I paid a very high price.'

The simple statement stunned her, and she shot to her feet. 'What do you mean? I was there, remember? No money changed hands.'

There was a cruel twist to his lips as he regarded her. 'There are more important things than money,' he said softly, and began to pack away the remains of their meal.

Alix watched him in mounting irritation. 'What does that mean? Damn you, Pierce, you can't possibly make a statement like that and not explain it.'

He laughed rather grimly. 'Haven't you learned yet that I can do anything I want to? Besides, you aren't yet ready to hear my explanation,' he commented over his shoulder. Ignoring her, he glanced up at the sun. 'It's about time we got on our way. We're going to be late as it is, and I don't want them sending out a search party.'

Balked by the wall he threw up, Alix could only choke on her anger. 'That would never do,' she sniped, and received an old-fashioned look for her pains.

'Don't be bitchy. You'll have me thinking you're frustrated.'

Alix ground her teeth. 'Sometimes I really loathe you, Pierce Martineau!'

Picking up the coolbox, he came across and held it out to her, yet didn't immediately release it when she took it. 'But what about the other times? What do you feel for me then, Alix?' he taunted softly.

God, he was impossible! 'Other times I try not to think of you at all!' she retorted, tugging at the box, which he finally let go.

He laughed low in his throat. 'Then there's hope for me yet. While you're still trying, I know you haven't succeeded,' he declared with satisfaction, and lowered his head towards hers.

Instantly Alix brought her free hand up to hold him off. 'You said you wouldn't lay a finger on me!' she reminded him, albeit far too breathlessly, and his smile widened.

He held his hands away from his body. 'Look, no hands,' he taunted, and ducked his head to take her parted lips in a kiss that stole her breath and sent liquid fire zinging along her veins. She trembled as his tongue sought hers, stroking until she could no longer hold back the response he demanded, and which her body ached to give. She knew that if she hadn't been holding the box nothing could have stopped her pressing herself closer. As it was, she was thankful she hadn't gone so far when Pierce drew back mere seconds later.

Blue eyes revealed leashed passion. 'I always keep my word, Alix...unless you want me to go on?'

She did want him to, and he knew it, and it was that which forced shaky legs to take a step backwards. 'You said we have to get back.'

He straightened, passion giving way to amusement. 'You could change my mind.'

Alix took in a wobbly breath. 'I don't want to.'

'One of these days I'm going to do what your eyes tell me, rather than your lips. And you know something, Alix? You won't even struggle,' he declared, and went to raise the anchor.

She was left gazing at his back, knowing it was true. It was getting harder and harder to fight when she was her own worst enemy. With a heavy sigh, she went below.

CHAPTER NINE

IT WAS almost dinnertime when they finally moored the yacht in the harbour. Pierce hadn't offered to let her have another attempt at steering, and Alix had been too sunk in her own thoughts to even dream of asking. She had had plenty to think about. A lot of things had finally become clear to her, but she felt as if she was locked in a game of pass the parcel. Only a small portion was revealed every time a layer was removed, and she had a growing presentiment that, when the final layer was removed, what it hid would prove to be vitally important.

There was no question about not believing his story regarding the shipping line. Thinking about it now, without the pain of his betrayal clouding her judgement, she knew Pierce had always spoken the truth. But, as she had told him, it didn't excuse what he had done. Yet even now that had become less clear. Adding it to what he had said about helping her father for her sake... suddenly she didn't know what to think. The edges of her anger had become blunted.

How she wished he had told her before, but honesty had her admitting that she wouldn't have believed him. He had said she wasn't ready to hear what he had to say, and she hadn't been. But she was getting there now. Even a week ago it would have been different, but now she wanted to listen... if only he would speak.

She stumbled as she stepped on to the jetty, and it was only Pierce's quick action which stopped her from hitting the concrete. He swept her up tightly to his firm body, so that Alix found her face pressed against his chest. She breathed in sharply, senses spinning at the heady mixture of sweat, salt, and his own particular scent. Swallowing hard, she looked up, straight into fathomless blue eyes, while their lips hovered only a tantalising breath apart.

'Are you OK?' Pierce asked, his voice sounding scratchy, and Alix forced a tense laugh from her tight throat.

'I don't think I've got my land legs back yet,' she joked, even as a devilish voice told her all she had to do was close that tiny gap and press her lips to his, and the long torment would be over.

'Then I'll just have to carry you, won't I?' he declared, fitting the action to the words before Alix could form a word of protest. Not that she would have done anyway. What energy she might have had to fight him must have drained away on the long trip home. She simply slipped her arms about his neck as he carried her to the buggy they had driven down in, giving herself up to the pleasure which being held so close afforded her.

Depositing her in her seat, Pierce remained leaning over her. 'Do I get a thank-you?' he asked softly, eyes dropping to her lips in a visual caress.

Alix suddenly decided she had had enough of thinking twice. This time she didn't think at all, just used the arm still circling his neck to pull his head down to hers, and brushing her lips over his. 'Will that do?' she queried, equally softly, and he straightened with a groan.

'Not by a long way, but here, in public, it's about all I can hope for,' he returned with gentle irony, and walked round to take his seat, leaving Alix with a soft flush warming her cheeks.

The journey up to the villa was short, just long enough for her to acknowledge that she had come a long way since yesterday, even from this morning, that she was openly contemplating things which she would have fought against tooth and nail only hours ago. Perhaps it was the island, or Pierce's relaxed hostility, but she knew she no longer cared as much about her pride. Somehow it was seeming to become not so important.

A visibly anxious Katina met them when they entered the villa, launching into a voluble flood of Greek which left Alix mystified and brought a deep frown to Pierce's forehead.

'Problems?' she asked, when the housekeeper went back to the kitchen.

'I hope not,' he answered, sounding thoughtful. 'The company have been trying to contact me, that's all. I'd better go and find out what it's all about.' Looking at her, and finally seeing her, he smiled. 'It shouldn't take long, then I'll join you for dinner.'

Alix watched him walk away, then headed for their bedroom. As she showered and changed, she was very much aware that they were at a turning-point. There was expectancy in the air, yet dared she make that vital move just on the evidence of one day? She wanted to, because she loved him, but she needed to know that he at least cared for her a little. So far there had been scant evidence of it, and that was why she hesitated still.

Although Pierce hadn't returned to the bedroom before she left it, he was not long in joining her in the lounge. However, he remained preoccupied throughout the meal. His replies to her attempts at conversation became increasingly monosyllabic, and Alix finally gave up. But the silence lengthened when they went out on to the terrace for coffee, and she found herself staring at Pierce's back as he stood staring broodingly out to sea. That was when she decided enough was enough.

'What's wrong, Pierce?' she asked, eyes running over the tense line of his back beneath his white dinner-jacket.

He must have been miles away, for he started at the sound of her voice, and turned to her with an apologetic smile. 'Sorry, was I ignoring you?'

Alix's teeth came together in a tiny irritated snap. 'Don't be so damned patronising. There's something wrong, isn't there? Can't you talk about it?'

Though his brows rose at her tone, he said nothing, merely came across to take the empty seat beside her, crossing one long leg over the other. 'There's nothing for you to trouble your head about. This is supposed to be a holiday.'

If he thought to divert her, it was the wrong tack to take. Her eyes narrowed. 'It's not a holiday, it's a honeymoon. I'm your wife,' she insisted, feeling a curling sensation in her stomach at the possessive sound of the words. 'If I can do nothing else, at least I can listen and try to ease the burden.'

Pierce stared down into his coffee, lips twisting. 'You pick a fine time to start asserting your position,' he retorted mockingly, and a shiver ran down her spine, for this was a return to the Pierce who had been conspicuously missing of late.

A conclusion which made her suddenly stop and think before jumping in with both feet. Something just didn't ring true, and her lips thinned as she realised what it was. 'You can't make me argue with you, Pierce. I *want* to know,' she declared firmly, and caught a flash of something like amusement in his eyes.

'Well, well, well, I knew there would come a time when you began to see through me, but I didn't reckon on tonight,' he revealed with a laugh of self-derision. 'All right, if you insist. There's been a slight hitch at one of our construction sites. It's one of my pet projects, so naturally I find it hard not being on hand to help.'

'What kind of hitch?'

Pierce scratched his forehead. 'There's some question as to who owns the land we're building on.'

Alix felt some of the tension leave her. 'That's it?' she asked dubiously. 'From your behaviour, I thought it was something more serious.'

He sent her a bland smile. 'Would I lie to you?'

That was a leading question if ever she'd heard one. 'Yes, if you had to. If you thought it necessary,' she declared, and knew at once that it was no more than the truth. Had probably always been the truth . . . and that should have told her something.

Pierce appeared to go quite still, but his eyes were watchful. 'Now there's an interesting statement. Do you think you're finally coming to understand me, Alix?'

She pulled a wry face, because for the first time in her life she was beginning to think she was. 'Wouldn't you say it was about time?' she mocked herself, even now needing some defence.

In answer Pierce dragged a hand through his hair, leaving it ruffled, so that Alix experienced a longing to go across and smooth it down. 'Many things are long overdue between us. What conclusions have you drawn?'

Alix glanced down at her hands. All she had to go on were feelings really. Pure feminine instinct. 'You're a very complicated man,' she declared, glancing at him through her lashes and seeing the way his lips twisted.

'As complicated as a Chinese puzzle,' he agreed, and Alix gave a tiny start of surprise.

'I had a Chinese puzzle once; it was very intricate. Then one day, by accident almost, I suddenly discovered the key to it, and of course I found it wasn't nearly so difficult at all. I could open it with my eyes shut,' she revealed, feeling strangely trembly inside, without knowing just why.

Pierce looked soberly back at her. 'It's a universal fact that the answer is always easy when you know it. The only hard questions are the ones you don't know the answers to.'

'Meaning there's a logical answer to everything?'

He spread his hands. 'Even me.'

Alix licked dry lips. This was a cat-and-mouse game with a difference. More was at stake here than just winning a battle of words. 'Which leaves me with two questions. Do I want to know the answer? And if so, how do I go about finding it?'

Pierce's face lost all signs of amusement as he observed her through narrowed eyes. 'Well, now, I can't help you with the first, but as to the second, how many clues do you need, Alix?' he demanded, with a decided edge to his voice which raised the lid on her own never far from boiling temper.

'How do I know, when you only give me half the facts?' she countered, feeling the moment was getting away from her just when she seemed to be making progress.

With an abrupt movement, Pierce rose to his feet. 'You don't want facts, Alix, you want assurances,' he returned curtly, and she shot up too.

'Is that a crime? Just what do you want of me, Pierce?' It was, if he only knew it, a cry from the heart.

'What do you want of *me*, Alix?' he countered softly, then, seeing her obvious confusion, sighed heavily. 'If you ever do decide, you know where to find me. I have to make another phone call. Excuse me.'

Alix watched him go with a sinking heart. They had been so close! She knew it in her bones. Yet . . . close to what? Her shoulders sagged. The answer to an unknown question. Why was he making everything so complicated? And yet hadn't she just said that the Chinese puzzle had been complicated until she knew the key? Which meant there was a simple answer to why he had gone to so much trouble to help her. But he could have done that just as easily without marrying her! Which could only mean he had *wanted* to marry her.

Her head began to thump and she clasped her hands to her temples. It didn't make sense. Didn't match up to what she had always known of him. Yet, only today, she had begun to discover that she hadn't really known him at all. Which meant. . .what? That nothing had been the way it seemed? Then or now? Yet there was no disguising the fact that he had hurt her so callously. It was hardly the action of a caring man. Until she recalled that he had helped her father when he hadn't had to.

Thoughts of her father brought her up short. She had meant to phone her mother when they arrived yesterday. She really ought to ring home. A glance at her watch told her it wasn't yet too late if she acted now. With that in mind she went in search of Pierce. As she had seen no sign of a telephone, then it must be in his study, wherever that was.

As it happened, she met him coming out of the room. 'Were you looking for me?' There was a sharp edge to the irony in his voice.

'Only indirectly. I wanted to use the phone to ring Mother. I meant to do it yesterday,' she explained, for some reason feeling extremely diffident. Perhaps it was the stern lines of his face which made her feel at fault somehow.

At her answer, however, the sternness vanished and mockery was back in his eyes. 'What else?' he drawled tiredly. With a studied show of gallantry he re-opened the door and switched on the light. 'Help yourself. The code is on the pad beside the phone.'

'Thank you,' she murmured politely as she passed by him, and he laughed shortly.

'Why thank me? It's your phone too. Everything here is yours now, sweet Alix. Give your mother my love, won't you?' he added, and closed the door after him.

Once again she was left staring after him. Everything here was hers? Did he include himself in that, and, if so, just what did he mean? She was beginning to feel hunted, as if he was laughing at her because, with all the clues he was giving her, she was still too blind to see the answer!

Irritated, she gave up and went to place her call. As she expected, her mother was still up, and they talked for almost an hour before Emily Petrakos exclaimed over the bill they were running up, and Alix felt compelled to say goodnight. She felt better for the call, even though it had solved nothing. But it was good to hear that her father was improving by the hour, now that he need worry no longer.

Sighing, she remained at the desk and took a curious glance about the room. It seemed to reflect Pierce's personality aptly—functional yet comfortable. The walls were lined with bookcases, some filled with books and others loaded with mementoes. There were the usual family photographs on one shelf, and she automatically rose and went over to it. There was a portrait of a man she recognised as Pierce's grandfather, but not the one he had once shown her at the New York apartment. The others must have been of various other members of his family. There was a wedding photo tucked in at the back too, and it came as a severe shock to realise it was of the two of them—yet nothing like the shock she felt next when it dawned on her that it was of their first wedding!

She stood there stunned. Pierce had kept a picture of them? Why, when by his own admission he had only married her to get the shipping line back? Why would a man bent on revenge do that, unless...? She shook her head in disbelief. No, it couldn't be. That would be too incredible! But even as she turned away her eye caught the title of one book, an anthology of poetry. She remembered he had referred to Lovelace only that afternoon, and she didn't hesitate to take the book and search the index.

Yet she hadn't needed to, because as she searched for the page the book fell open of its own accord. And there was a poem, its last lines underlined in red.

I could not love thee (Dear) so much, Lov'd I not honour more.

Love? Honour? She held on to the bookcase as her legs felt weak. Had he, all this time, been trying to tell her that he loved her? That he had always loved her? She doubted her own reasoning, and yet, amazingly, everything suddenly seemed to fit into place. His reasons for helping her family, and for insisting on marriage. All done because he loved her?

How she longed to believe it, but she had been hurt very badly once for believing he loved her. She didn't think she could go through that again and survive. Yet what other explanation fitted the circumstances? But if he loved her, why hadn't he told her? Because he had his pride, too. Even the bravest man must fear rejection, and she had given him no reason to suppose that she would welcome a declaration of love from him. On the contrary, she had been quick to hurt lest she be hurt, so he had told her she wasn't ready to hear him. All he had done was give her a rose and jokingly say he might have given it to lay his heart symbolically at her feet, for her to trample over in her turn!

Oh, Pierce!

Of course, she could be wrong, but she had to know. One way or the other, finally she had to know, because her whole future depended on it. Hastily she put the book back, turning off the light as she left, heading for the terrace. Only Pierce wasn't there, nor was he in the lounge. That only left their bedroom.

She found him there, the low glow of one lamp revealing his long figure standing out on the balcony, a towel hitched low about his hips, and his hair shining wetly, evidence that he had just come from the shower. For an instant she hesitated, then kicked off her shoes and padded across the carpet to him. She halted a breath away, yet not by a flicker did he show he had heard her.

There was something forbidding in the set of his back, but she refused to be put off. She licked her lips. 'Pierce?' Her voice was a low croak which she barely heard herself. Yet he stiffened, his whole attitude now one of waiting. She spoke again, and this time she reached out to touch his shoulder. 'Pierce?'

His reaction was electric. With a groan he spun round, reaching for her and pulling her into his arms. 'Thank God. You're a hard woman, Alix. I thought you'd never come!' he growled emotively, and lowered his head.

Heart in her throat, her hands came up to his shoulders, her intention to hold him off as she denied him. 'No. Don't Pierce, I——' The rest of the words died under his mouth.

He kissed her with a searing passion that allowed no room for protest. She did try to struggle, but it was a half-hearted attempt at best, because her hands betrayed her, clutching on to the hot silken skin beneath them and urging him closer. Pierce's triumphant grunt of satisfaction made her stomach clench in response, and she discovered that the strange whimpering sounds she could hear were her own as she kissed him back with equal passion.

When at last he tore his mouth from hers, she dragged air into her desperately panting lungs. A remnant of sanity remained. 'Pierce . . . wait!'

His head came up, eyes burning hotly into hers. 'It's too late for waiting, Alix. We both want this, don't we?' he demanded gruffly, and her throat closed over.

He was right. What good were words when they could communicate like this? The reason for her being there vanished under a more urgent need. 'Yes,' she groaned, 'we both want it.'

Immediately she lost her breath again as his lips trailed moistly down her tense throat to claim the rapid pulse at it base. 'I need you, Alix. God, how I need you tonight!' he breathed against her, and at that desperately wanted admission she was lost.

She was scarcely aware of his hands deftly removing her clothes from her until he broke contact long enough to carry her to the bed and laid her down, tossing the towel away before joining her. The sensation of flesh on flesh drove every other thought from her head. It felt right, it felt good, and her body flowered as she longed to be closer to his dizzying heat. His hand traced the graceful line of her thigh upwards, across her fluttering stomach, until it found and claimed her breast. His mouth followed, teasing the turgid peak with lips and teeth before drawing her into his mouth. Her head went back, eyes closing as she couldn't help but press her quivering flesh against the source of such devastatingly bewitching torture.

Crazy or not, she wanted this. Wanted it with a desperation which turned her body molten and started up an aching throb deep within her. All her movements were jerky and uncoordinated as she finally allowed herself to respond in the way she had longed to do since the moment she realised she still loved him. The feel of his solid flesh against hers was dizzying, and the thrusting evidence of Pierce's arousal made her groan and move against him in an invitation as old as time itself.

When his head lifted, she let out a moan of protest, but it was only so that he could work the same nerve-tensing pleasure on her other breast. His tongue stroked and teased until she was ready to scream, but it was the greedy suckling which followed that took her voice as her hips arched against his, moving with an urgency that she no longer cared about. She was wild for him, wanted to feel him inside her, filling her, taking away the emptiness and loneliness of the past years. She thrust her fingers into his hair, dragging his head up to hers to tell him so, but before she could utter a syllable his mouth claimed hers again, tongue thrusting in an erotic parody which she met and matched feverishly.

She was burning up with need, and her every movement told him so. Yet she barely registered the long caress of his hand along her thigh, or its journey upwards again to the moist core of her. Only when his hand closed possessively around her and his fingers began a stroking caress did she gasp. She wanted to protest that this wasn't what she wanted, but already her body was tensing, coiling as he expertly urged her towards the peak she so desperately sought.

Even as partial release caught her with a sobbing cry Pierce moved over her, easing her thighs apart and entering her with compelling mastery. Breathlessly she rose to meet his thrusts, and in wonder felt that coil of tension begin to grow, yet deeper and more powerful this time, as he filled her, making her his in the most intimate way of all.

Their need was too violent for the moment to last long, and they climaxed within seconds of each other. With a shuddering cry, Pierce collapsed on to her, and, dazed as she was by a pleasure so complete, she still welcomed him, arms curving possessively about his heaving shoulders. She didn't want to think, just wanted to hold on to him. What they had just shared had been wild and wonderful. There would be time enough later for all the questions.

Pierce's breathing settled, and she wondered if he had fallen asleep. Her eyes closed too, but after a while his weight began to feel uncomfortable, and, taking care, she tried to ease out from beneath him only to feel one large hand close about her hip as he tensed.

'No!' he muttered against her skin, the words coming from him as if they were driven. 'I'm not going to lose you again.'

Alix gasped at the barely audible admission. Her heart swelled inside her, and sudden tears welled behind her eyes. To hear her supremely self-confident husband say that filled the aching void. He cared. He had to. But was it love? She didn't know, but right now what she had was enough. Because until now she had had nothing.

Consequently, her voice was low and husky as she said, 'I'm not going anywhere. You're just too heavy.'

Still more asleep than awake, he eased off her with a muttered, 'Sorry,' but he took her with him, curling her into the curves of his body and holding her there with his arm.

Alix had never felt more cherished or secure. Home was in his arms whether he loved her or not, but she hoped to God that he did love her, because she could no longer hide her love for him. Her lashes dropped once more. Tomorrow she would know. Tomorrow.

They were awoken in the morning by a strangely familiar noise. Pierce stirred first, and it was his movements which brought Alix back reluctantly to the land of the living. She was still lying in his arms, but even as the sight of their naked bodies, intimately entwined together, brought memories of the night Pierce was easing away from her and leaving the bed. Coming up on her elbow, she focused blearily on his straight back as he went to the window.

'What is it?' she asked, not quite functioning enough to make the identification, yet well enough to appreciate the taut curve of his buttocks and the muscles in his thighs. A cat-like smile tilted her lips as she imagined her hands running over them, which they could do, if he would only come back to bed.

Pierce heaved a deep sigh, and squared his shoulders. 'It's the helicopter,' he informed her in a grim voice, which instantly banished the state of delicious lethargy she had been happy to bask in, making her sit up and take notice.

A tiny frown cut into her forehead as she realised he didn't seem in the least surprised by the arrival. On the contrary. 'Were you expecting it?'

Turning away from the window, Pierce dragged both hands through his hair and reached for his robe. 'I arranged for it last night, but I didn't expect to oversleep this morning.'

The fact that he had known, yet said nothing, brought an unnamed fear to chill her blood. Alix found that her mouth had gone dry. 'Why is it here?' she asked in a voice that croaked.

Pierce glanced at her briefly. 'I'm afraid the honeymoon is over, Alix,' he told her flatly, and it was the very lack of emotion as he spoke which made her heart kick in sudden inexplicable anxiety.

It was like *déjà vu*, as if the events of five years ago were happening all over again. Yet she refused to give in to the panic which hovered on the edges of her consciousness. She was not yet ready to accept that last night had meant nothing.

'What does that mean?' she demanded, grateful to hear that the words didn't waver and betray her.

Pierce spoke through a tightly set jaw. 'It means you'd better get dressed and pack a case. The rest can be sent on later.'

Her heart lurched on a dizzying wave of relief. Dear lord, he had almost scared her rigid! A shaky laugh left her. 'You mean it's come for us? Tell me where we're going, so I know what to pack.'

His head came up, and the breath he took hissed in through his teeth. '*You'll* be on a flight back to England.'

She couldn't have felt more shocked if he'd actually hit her, and Alix's fingers clutched at the sheet. 'You're sending me away?' she charged dazedly, unable to take her eyes from his.

His nod of assent was abrupt. 'You'd better get moving. Time is short, and we've wasted enough of it already.'

Wasted time? Was he saying that all that loving was wasted time? It was another blow, but this time it had the effect of snapping her out of the shock. She would not let history repeat itself. This time she refused to be dismissed so callously. 'Why?'

'Why what?' he countered irritably, and she felt a ball of anger begin to swell inside her.

'Why are you sending me away?' she enlarged bitingly, and drew hooded eyes to her pale face.

'Because I have things to do, and I don't want you here getting in the way.'

It would have been so easy, in that instant, to let her emotions rule her actions, but she was older and wiser now. There were bells ringing in her head, and one of them didn't ring true. Things to do? What things? Until last night, this had been simply a honeymoon. Now, this morning, he was dismissing her. What had happened in between?

Then, of course, she knew. 'You lied to me, didn't you? There was more to that phone call yesterday than you said,' she charged, hating the way he had shut her out, was still shutting her out. 'That's what this is really all about, isn't it? Why couldn't you tell me? Don't I have a right to know?'

Meeting the accusation in her grey eyes, Pierce snapped tight the belt he was tying. 'There was no point in alarming you unnecessarily,' he said shortly, and her heart immediately jumped into her throat.

'You think it was less alarming to be told to pack and go?' she countered angrily, scrambling from the bed and grabbing her own robe.

'What I was hoping to do was avoid just this sort of pointless argument,' he gritted back tensely.

'Pointless?' she queried with a hint of mockery. 'I think it's very much to the point. How can I trust you when you treat me like this? What aren't you telling me about this "little hitch"?'

Pierce's gaze became glacial. 'I've told you all you need to know,' he insisted stonily, but that only inflamed her anger.

'You've told me all you *want* me to know, and that's something entirely different! What will you be doing when I'm conveniently out of the way?'

He clearly didn't like her sarcasm. 'I have a short trip of my own to make. It's business, and I don't need you along,' he said acidly.

'Which means it's dangerous, whatever it is,' she deduced, cold fingers running up her spine. What on earth was going on?

'Crossing the street is dangerous, if you don't watch what you're doing,' he returned brusquely, doubling her alarm, not easing it in the slightest.

His 'little woman' attitude infuriated her, and hurt her too. She deserved better than that from him. Stamping across to him, her hands caught hold of his lapels. 'Stop treating me like a foolish child, Pierce. Tell me where you're going!'

His hands came up to fasten over hers, but made no move to remove them. 'It would make no difference if I told you.'

Her eyes searched his and met an infuriatingly blank wall. Yet when it came to stubbornness she had her fair share too. 'OK, don't tell me, but I'm your wife, Pierce Martineau, and I've been crossing streets safely for years. Wherever you're going, I'm going with you!'

In an instant the air between them fairly sizzled with tension. The wall came down with a crash, revealing a volcanic rage, and his hands tightened punishingly on her wrists. 'Like hell you are! You're going nowhere.'

Alix raised her chin pugnaciously. 'Try and stop me!'

Pierce visibly conquered his anger, eyes taking on a mocking gleam. 'What is this? You've been trying to get away from me for weeks, now you're clinging like a limpet. What happened?'

The return of the mockery she hated was a calculated slap in the face, but she refused to back off, recognising it for the deliberate ploy it was. 'Last night happened, or had you forgotten?' she reminded him softly.

He drew in an audible breath at that, the lines of his face setting deep and grim. 'Low blow, Alix,' he declared curtly.

'You started this, with your commands! Well, I won't be ordered about without reason. A marriage should be a partnership. I'm not weak, I can take the truth. I deserve it. I'm going with you because you haven't given me one good reason why I shouldn't!' she argued defiantly.

Releasing her hands and grabbing her shoulders, he gave her a shake. 'Listen, you little fool, the only danger is that while I'm arguing with you the fault isn't being put right!'

'Then stop arguing,' she advised shortly.

Swearing under his breath, he flung her away, stepping back from her. 'I don't have time for this. You aren't going, and that's final.'

Hurt and anger filled her in equal parts. This was now a matter of principle. Either they had a marriage or they didn't. He couldn't just order her about without explanation. If he expected her to trust him, then she had the right to the truth. Damn him, couldn't he also see how worried she was? Everything he wasn't saying just made her anxiety grow! If something was wrong, she wanted to help. If there was danger involved, then she wanted to share it. Damn it, she loved him, and she would not sit calmly by and let him walk into the lion's den alone!

It was the merging of all her love and fear which produced her next statement.

'Make me leave here without a good reason, Pierce, and you'll never see me again!' The rash challenge was as much a shock to Alix as the words tumbled out as they were to Pierce, who went rigid as a statue.

'Threats, Alix?' he countered dulcetly, and her nerves jolted.

She was white as a sheet, but it was impossible to retract the words once said, although she instantly regretted them. She knew it was the wrong tack to take, but she had wanted him to talk to her, not close himself off! Now, having started, she had to go on. 'I won't be shut out!'

'And I won't be coerced.'

She swallowed hard. 'Then it's stalemate, isn't it?'

Pierce's smile was chilling. 'Not quite. You still have to pack. From the mainland, you'll have no trouble picking up a flight to England.'

She couldn't believe he was calling her bluff. 'So it's over, just like that?' she declared gruffly.

'Your decision, Alix.'

She stared at him, heart thudding so loudly that she was sure he must hear it. Where had all the warmth and promise of the night gone? How on earth had they come to this so suddenly? She felt sick, desperately wishing she could take everything back, but finding the words choked her. 'No, it was your decision. It doesn't have to come to this.'

'It already has.'

Hot tears burned the backs of her eyes, but she refused to let a single one drop. 'So last night meant nothing to you?'

Something flickered in his eyes for a moment. 'On the contrary, you could call it the perfect farewell. Now, unless you have anything further to say, I'd better go and see who arrived.' Without another word, he turned away, his thoughts already very far from her as he strode from the room.

In a state of shock she simply stood staring at the closed door. She could scarcely credit that he had accepted her ultimatum. Surely he must have known she wasn't serious, that it was just a spur-of-the-moment thing? Shaky legs took her to the bed, where she sat down gratefully. She didn't know how it had all happened so fast. From insisting she would go with him, suddenly the marriage was over and she was on her way home!

It was like a nightmare. Everything seemed distorted. Last night she had believed she had finally understood, and then this had happened. Why? Damn him! Why had he so stubbornly refused to tell her where he was going, and why? Shock rapidly gave way to anger as she dwelt on the last few minutes. No. She was damned if she'd go! Not without a suitable explanation. Last night he had said he wouldn't let her go, and now he was quietly telling her to go? It didn't make sense.

Except, of course, it did, as soon as she made the contradiction. She gasped aloud. He had, she realised now, very neatly used her own anger against her, and she had come within an ace of letting him win. The knowledge revitalised her flagging spirit.

Gritting her teeth, she went to the dressing-room to grab up some clothes and headed for the bathroom. She showered and dressed in jeans and shirt in next to no time, and didn't bother to do more than run a brush through her hair. She couldn't afford the time, because whatever Pierce said she was determined to stay right where she was. She did pack a case, though, and left it on the bed with her bag. She would need it, but not to go to England.

So, much less than ten minutes later, she walked into the lounge, ready to do battle, to find that Pierce had somehow found the time to dress too, and was now in deep conversation with a tall fair-haired man. They both looked round as she entered, and her husband's face was set in stern lines as he beckoned her over.

'Alix, this is Pat Denning, my right-hand man,' he introduced them in an icy voice.

'Pleased to meet you at last, Mrs Martineau,' Pat Denning declared in a friendly Texas drawl, shaking hands with her, his smile faintly tense. 'I'm sorry to have to drag you away from your husband.'

She returned his smile with an edged one of her own. 'That's OK, because I'm not going anyway.'

Beside her Pierce breathed in harshly. 'I thought we'd settled all that,' he ground out tersely.

Alix shrugged, although it took quite an effort to make it careless. 'I was lying and you know it.'

Their eyes engaged in silent battle, with neither looking away. Pierce set his jaw. 'I wasn't,' he returned, but she simply raised her chin. 'For God's sake, Alix, don't force me to do something I'll regret!' he warned coldly.

Her expression became every bit as stubborn as he might have expected. 'I don't believe you've regretted anything in your life! And I refuse to go until you explain why I should.'

Again that nerve ticked in his jaw. 'What are you trying to get me to say, Alix? That I've had all I wanted from you, and now you can go? Well, if that's what it takes, consider it said!'

She felt her blood seethe with anger at the studied cruelty of the words. Five years ago she might have believed him, but with her fledgeling insight she saw something in the peculiar tension filling him which made her stick her chin out once more. 'I don't believe you,' she returned softly, 'and the only way you'll get me off this island is if you knock me senseless.'

Pierce swore long and hard.

Pat Denning's slow drawl broke the silence. 'It's getting late, boss,' he interjected.

The comment brought Alix's head round towards him, and in the next split-second she heard Pierce mutter, 'Oh, hell!' and, turning back, came into sharp contact with his fist. Blackness opened at her feet and she plunged headlong into it.

Pierce caught her as she fell, as white now as she was. 'She's OK. I pulled my punch. Her bag's in the bedroom; get it, will you, while I put her in the helicopter?' Face set in grim lines, he carried her outside to where the steel bird waited, strapping her into the machine, and tenderly probing the darkening spot on her chin. 'Damn you, Alix, must you fight me all the time?' he muttered, then turned as Pat Denning came to climb in.

He looked questioningly at his employer. 'Sure you want it this way, boss?'

'Just get her out of here, will you, Pat? Make sure she's safe.'

Pat signalled to the pilot, then raised his voice over the mounting engine noise. 'I'll do that, but I sure wouldn't want to be in your shoes when you get back! See ya, boss.'

CHAPTER TEN

ALIX returned to consciousness with a groan. Her jaw ached like the very devil and her head seemed to be thumping outrageously.

'You OK there, ma'am?'

The drawled query from beside her brought her head up and round, and she realised the thumping sensation came from the fact that she was airborne in a helicopter. Then, of course, she recalled everything—her refusal to leave, Pierce's warning, and the final indignity of the way he had knocked her out.

With a cry which made her jaw ache further, she looked around. Ahead of her sat the pilot, beside her lounged a blonde giant, and through the window she could see the island and the sparkling blue waters surrounding it. She could also see the speck that was Pierce watching them leave, and her hands went instantly to the belt which held her in place, wrenching at it in her efforts to break free. She would jump out and swim back! She'd...

Strong hands clamped down on hers, stilling her movements. 'Whoa there, ma'am. Pierce wants you alive, not throwing yourself from a moving helicopter and killing yourself!'

Alix turned angrily flashing eyes on her guardian. 'Who the hell are you?' she demanded, then winced, raising a hand to cradle her jaw.

The giant whistled silently. 'Pat Denning. We *were* introduced. You're going to have a bruise the size of a hen's egg, I'm afraid,' he observed sympathetically.

'He hit me!' The statement was a mixture of anger and disbelief.

'Seemed to think it was the only thing he could do. I figured it was a big mistake, but he knows you better than I do.'

'I'm going to kill him!' Alix declared wrathfully, trying, without much success, to get her brain working. It was one thing to invite him to do it, another for him to take up the option!

'Figured you might want to do that,' Pat Denning agreed laconically.

Even in the depths of her anger Alix was tempted to laugh, but she gritted her teeth. 'Take me back to the island,' she ordered instead.

'Can't do that, ma'am. I have my orders,' he refused in his friendly way, and she sent him a flashing look.

'Where is he going?' she demanded, determined to get a flight there somehow.

Ruefully, Pat Denning shook his head. 'Sorry, I can't tell you that.'

Her look became derisive. 'Is there anything you *can* tell me?'

He gave that some thought. 'Figure not.'

That had her lip curling sarcastically. 'You do a lot of figuring, don't you? Is that what Pierce hired you for?'

'Guess so,' he agreed.

'That and kidnapping women, to be more exact.'

Pat Denning turned to frown at her over that remark. 'You want to be careful, ma'am. Saying things like that can get a man into a powerful lot of trouble.'

Having calmed down, Alix found she was beginning to get the measure of this man. 'Exactly. So now are you going to tell me where Pierce is going?' she bartered, knowing she didn't have to spell everything out.

She received a look of considerable respect. 'You play a mean game, ma'am. Hell, the truth is, Pierce isn't going anywhere,' he pronounced bluntly.

She hadn't been expecting that. 'What do you mean? What about the construction company?'

Pat sent her a wry smile. 'Oh, the company is building a dam in one of those tiny little Central American states all right, but that has nothing to do with this. Some lunatic with a grudge took a pot-shot at his brother in Italy, day before yesterday. Missed, thank the good lord, but he disappeared, and we think he's on the way to try to get Pierce. The plan is for Pierce to stay put, and the police will catch him as he makes his move.' Hearing her gasp, he sent her a solemn look. 'Figured you had a right to know, ma'am.'

Alix swallowed back a sudden rush of nausea as she thought of Pierce staying in the danger area. Staking himself out like a Judas goat, just waiting to be killed! 'Why didn't he tell me?' she croaked out of a dry throat, willing herself not to utter the scream which grew inside her.

'Said he didn't want you to worry.'

'Not worry?' she ejaculated. How on earth could he think she'd worry less not knowing the facts? Was he crazy? 'He should have told me!'

'Reckon he should at that. Told him so, but he wouldn't listen. Said you'd insist on staying behind, and he wanted you safely off the island.'

'Oh, God!' Alix had to acknowledge that Pierce was right. She would have refused to go. But that didn't alter the fact that he should have told her the truth.

'Don't be too hard on him, ma'am. Poor old Pierce never could think straight where you were concerned,' Pat enlarged, squeezing her hand avuncularly, although he was much the same age as Pierce.

Alix frowned, tearing her gaze from the window and the rapidly decreasing island. 'What do you mean?'

He shrugged and pulled a wry face. 'Where would I start? Take that business of the shipping line. We all told him he could get it for a tenth of the price, but would he listen? Uh-uh. He paid the full market price as if they were seaworthy, and then put in the same amount to bring them up to scratch. Crazy! But he wouldn't hear any argument.'

Alix didn't know whether she was on her head or her heels. 'Are we talking about the Petrakos shipping line?' she queried, and when he nodded went on stiltedly, 'But he got that for nothing.' I know, I was there! she thought grimly. She would never forget; it was etched indelibly into her memory.

'Hate to argue with a lady, but you're wrong, ma'am. I helped draw up the papers, and witnessed the bill of sale,' he corrected, watching that fact sink in.

Alix sank into silence, everything she had thought she understood suddenly plunged into turmoil. Pierce had bought the ships. He had gone back and bought them! But why? Why, when he already had them for nothing? It didn't make sense, but now she understood why he said he had paid a high price for the line. According to Pat Denning, it had been very high indeed.

Her grandfather had never told her, she thought achingly. He had known how being used had hurt her, yet she now knew he had cared more for his money than her sense of self-worth, which a simple word could have restored. All these years she had thought Pierce had bartered her, and her grandfather had allowed her to believe it because he could not stand the thought of her loving an Andreas!

'Thank you for telling me, Pat,' she murmured gruffly.

'I only hope it helps, because I'd hate to see Pierce hurting the way he was before. He had us all worried, working like the devil until he was nothing but skin and bones. All he'd say was it was his fault you'd left and this was the only way to put it right. I thought it had worked, too, when he finally told me he'd married you. Wouldn't be surprised, though, if he's not thinking he's probably scuppered his chances again.'

'Why would he think that?'

'Seems to me it would take a certain kind of woman to forgive the man who'd knocked her cold.' He sent her a quizzical look, eyebrows raised.

Alix couldn't laugh, not with Pierce back on the island waiting for some madman to turn up and shoot him! 'How can I forgive him if he's dead?' she demanded thickly, voice wavering with mounting dread.

'Don't book the wake too soon, ma'am. Pierce doesn't aim to get shot. You'll have your chance to murder him!'

Alix found she was gripping his hand tightly. 'Please, God!'

'Amen to that.'

Once more she looked out of the window, but now there was nothing to see. Fear clutched at her heart. 'What am I going to do?'

'The best thing you can do is what Pierce wants. He doesn't need to be worrying about you too. Go to England, and wait there.'

Alix swallowed hard. Wait? What else could she do, except wait and pray?

Twenty-four hours later, Alix paced once more to the window, wondering if she was beginning to wear a furrow in the carpet of the flat above Pierce's office in the Martineau building. Contrary to expectations, she had not gone to England. Oh, Pat Denning had ushered her to the airport all right, but he had had to get away again, so he never knew that she changed the ticket he had given her for a seat on a jet bound for New York.

She hadn't told him because she hadn't been prepared to argue about it. All she did know was that any news about Pierce would go to head office first, and that building was in New York. Her initial plan had been to use Pierce's apartment, despite the bad memories it held for her, and haunt his office from there. But the apartment had proved to be empty, and had been so for quite some time, according to a neighbour. Balked, she had been about to go to a hotel when she remembered Pierce saying there was an apartment above his office at the Martineau building. It was late when she arrived, but the security guard had been only too happy to let her in when he discovered who she was.

Then the waiting had begun. The flight had been a tense one, but at least she had been doing something; now all she could do was sit back and twiddle her

thumbs. There hadn't been anyone she could talk to
without spreading alarm, and common sense told her
that rumours could spread all too easily. All she had
been able to do was contact his secretary, inventing a
shopping trip, and asking her to have Pierce phone the
apartment if he should get in touch. But no call had
come all day, and now she found herself swallowing back
the gnawing anxiety which sometimes threatened to
engulf her.

Where was he? *How* was he?

Now, just when she needed to see him, needed to hear
his voice, the silence was appalling. It didn't matter if
she never heard him explaining what Pat Denning had
told her, never heard him saying what she was truly becoming to believe he felt for her. She just needed to know
he was alive.

Where they went from there she didn't know. There
was so much to explain, and she didn't dare think too
far ahead. She had gone that course once, and it had
ended in rejection. Yet that, too, now needed to be explained. Why had he done it? Why had he done all the
things he had? It seemed she had a million questions,
and no husband to supply the answers.

With a nervous gesture, she pulled the cord which
closed the curtains. Her stomach rumbled, and she
realised she had eaten nothing since breakfast. She hadn't
fancied food then any more than she did now. Common
sense told her it would be silly to make herself ill, so she
went to the kitchen and fixed herself a sandwich and
some coffee. She attempted to eat it while watching television, but that was too trivial for her to concentrate on,
and she eventually gave up.

Although a yawn overtook her, Alix knew she was too worried to sleep—especially in that big bed which was designed for two, and only seemed to emphasise her loneliness. Avoiding looking at it, she went to shower, afterwards wrapping herself in an ankle-length silk robe before padding back to the lounge. There was an old movie on the TV, and she switched it over, watching as the darkness settled about her, curled up in one corner of the couch. Gradually, though, sheer exhaustion had her lids growing heavy, and without really realising it she fell into a doze.

It was the bright flash of light against her eyelids which stirred her several hours later, and she squinted, blinking awake, staring at the tall figure who stood in the doorway as if he were a ghost.

'Alix?' Her name was a disbelieving croak on Pierce's lips, and she sat up, suddenly wide awake. He looked exhausted, the growth of beard heavy on his chin, and his clothes looking as if they had been slept in for several days and nights. But, dear lord, he had never looked so wonderful.

'What are you doing here?' he asked gruffly before she could find a single thing to say.

At the sight of him, Alix's heart had trebled its beat. She had been on the point of rushing across the floor and flinging herself into his arms, but there was something in the way he was standing which rooted her to the spot. 'I went to the apartment, but it was empty. I remembered you mentioning this, and your security man let me in,' she explained inanely, licking dry lips.

Across the room, Pierce shook his head dazedly. 'I gave it up,' he informed her in a strange voice, even as his eyes were eating her up—as if he had never expected to see her again.

Alix had the weirdest feeling that she was watching two other people acting out a scene from a play, speaking lines which were a million miles away from what they were really feeling. 'Why?'

'I couldn't live in it after you left. Couldn't live with the memory of what happened there,' Pierce declared, then seemed to give one almighty shudder, as if waking up from an unpleasant dream. Dropping the case he had still been holding, he pushed the door closed and took a step forward. 'Alix, for God's sake, what are you doing *here*?' he repeated the question in a sharp tone, making her jump.

She struggled to her feet, brushing down the silky material of her robe with hands that shook. This wasn't going at all the way she expected. 'I told you. I couldn't use the apart——'

The words cut off as he closed the gap between them in three strides, taking her by the shoulders and shaking her. 'Not here. In America. You were supposed to be in England!'

Blinking at the note of angry despair in his voice, she cleared her throat nervously. 'I know, but it was too far away! I came here because I thought this was where any news would come first. I needed to know you were all right,' she explained quickly, amazed to see the colour wash in and out of his face.

He let her go then, dragging his hands down his face in a tired gesture which twisted her heart. His laugh was harshly self-mocking. 'Dear God, have you any idea how I felt when I got to England and you weren't there? When nobody knew where you were? I was back in hell again, and didn't think I could stand it, and all the while you were here, waiting for news of me!'

Alix was stunned at the sick look which had passed across his face when he spoke of hell. 'I . . . didn't know.'

Her answer was soft, but she doubted if he would have heard it if she had shouted, for he was lost somewhere in his own far from pleasant memories. 'Hell, I knew I'd ruined my chances of ever getting you back, really back, when I had to hit you, but I had to try again anyway.' He laughed humourlessly. 'When you weren't there, I nearly went out of my mind!' Now he looked at her and really saw her, looking at him in a kind of stunned trance. 'Damn you, Alix, when are you going to realise that I love you?' he demanded in a voice loud enough to raise the dead.

There was a moment when the room swam alarmingly, but she got herself together, knowing this was definitely not the time to faint. 'When you tell me,' she said huskily, then got angry. 'Damn you, Pierce, I'm not clairvoyant. I need to be told these things!' she cried, and his head went back as he froze, eyes locking into hers.

'I just did.'

'I heard you.'

She didn't just see him swallow, she heard him. 'And?'

She knew what he wanted to hear, but the words hesitated on her lips. She was afraid to admit her feelings, commit herself, when she had been hurt before. At her silence, Pierce's face broke up, and he swung away from her, pacing to stand before the now silent television.

'I gave up the right to hear you say you love me a long time ago, didn't I?' he challenged thickly. 'Lord, the gods were really laughing when they gave me you to love!'

The bitter anger and despair in his voice tore her heart apart. 'Don't, Pierce!' she cried in distress, then gasped as he turned a chalk-white face to her.

'Don't what? Hate myself? But who else can I blame, Alix? Who else hurt you? Who else twisted the knife in you and killed the best thing that had ever happened to him? I was guilty and I deserved every bit of the punishment I got. I loved you when I married you. I loved you even when I was destroying you, and I've loved you every day since. I'll love you till the day I die.'

Alix didn't know she was crying, but the tears were streaming down her cheeks as she shook her head helplessly. 'Then why?'

There was no need for her to say more. Pierce closed his eyes in pain, then came to her, pulling her resistless body into his arms, cradling her head with hands that trembled. 'Because I met you too late,' he confessed hoarsely. His sigh was made of the tiredness of long years. 'My grandfather made me promise on his deathbed that I would be revenged on Yannis Petrakos. That I would, by whatever means I had to, get our ships back. I gave my word, Alix, long before I ever knew you existed.

'I cannot excuse what I did. When I knew a granddaughter existed, and having failed to buy back the ships by all legal means, I decided to use her to get them by blackmail. Honour demanded it. Try to understand. I knew that if there was one thing Petrakos would hate it was knowing his granddaughter had been dishonoured by a member of my family. I knew he would give anything to have that wiped out, and my price would be the fleet. It was cold-blooded but simple...only I hadn't met you then.

'When I did, I fell in love with you on sight. You were so lovely. So innocent, yet generous—everything I had ever hoped to find in the woman I loved. I was tormented. I would have given everything I possessed to change things, but I couldn't. My word had been given. Though I suffered the tortures of hell in doing it, I carried out the plan. All I could do for you was do what had to be done in such a way to make you hate me—hate me so much you'd be damned if you let me affect your life from that day on. You say I killed something fine that day—well, something died in me too. I had no hope of regaining what I had destroyed, yet I couldn't let you go. I promised myself that I would watch over you, help you if you ever needed it, and perhaps even one day win the right to your love again.'

As Alix listened, so much became clear. If she believed him—and how could she not after that heartfelt confession?—then he had been hurting just as she had. It was not an excuse, it was fact. He accepted blame, lived with it daily, but knowledge could not conquer hope entirely. Didn't she know exactly how that felt? Raising her head at last, she looked deeply into his blue eyes.

'That's why you married me?'

He nodded. 'And why your freedom is yours if you ask for it,' he added solemnly.

Now it was Alix's turn to ease away, eyes dropping to where she could see his pulse beating erratically at the open neck of his shirt. 'You must have loved your grandfather very much.'

Pierce hesitated fractionally before saying, 'I did, but not in the same way that I love you. What can I say? I knew him before you. He raised my family when our parents died. He had first call on my loyalty.'

Alix had lived all her life with that Greek sense of family honour. She could understand it, even if she could not condone it. Pierce had used her to settle a debt, and, having done so, given that loyalty to her. Now she fully understood that reference to Lovelace. Were he not such an honourable man, he could not love her as much as he did.

She raised her eyes. 'I should hate you.'

Pierce tipped his head in acknowledgement. 'I deserve it.'

'I should be telling you that I'll never forgive you.'

Blue eyes lasered into hers. 'And are you telling me that, Alix?'

Again she held back, not ready yet to commit herself fully. 'How can I be sure something like that won't happen again?'

'Because I'd cut off my right arm rather than let any harm come to you, either through me or anyone else,' Pierce returned forcefully, such a power in his determination that a shiver of awareness ran through her.

She couldn't resist raising a contemplative hand to her chin. 'To the extent of knocking me out?'

Pierce stiffened, rueful eyes dropping to her chin, and his hand lifted to brush hers away and run tenderly over the faint bruising. 'I wanted you safe, Alix,' he pointed out gruffly, and she sighed.

'You could have tried talking to me, Pierce.'

'I didn't think you'd listen. You see, I assumed you felt the same way I did. If you were going anywhere dangerous, I'd be sticking to you like glue. Was I wrong?'

he challenged, eyes softening as colour stole into her cheeks.

'No,' she admitted, then, seeing the way his gaze had fallen intently on her lips, feeling them tingle as if his own had actually brushed them, she raised a hand to his mouth, holding him at bay. 'Did they get the man? Are you safe now?'

'Pat told you?'

'He thought I had a right to know. I did, but I'd rather have heard it from you, Pierce.'

He sighed. 'Forgive me, but all I could think of was getting you off the island.'

'And you weren't hurt?' Her eyes scanned all she could see for signs of a wound.

'The police got the man before he even got close to me. I would have come here sooner, but there were questions to be answered, and I had to talk to my brother.'

'I didn't know you had a brother,' she said, wondering if they would ever really communicate, when such basic knowledge was missing.

Pierce smiled, as if reading her mind. 'When you and I are together, ordinary conversation seems unnecessary. But I promise not to hide anything from you again. I've a brother and two sisters, all waiting to meet you at last.'

Alix was surprised. 'You mean they know about me?'

He shrugged. 'Everything. We're very close. They helped to keep me going when times got bad. My sisters are hoping you'll finally stop hating me.'

That brought up another question. 'If you were so determined to make me hate you when you used me to get the shipping line, why did you go back and buy them?'

'Pat again,' he acknowledged ruefully.

'Don't blame him, he was trying to help,' she said quickly, then frowned. 'Weren't you afraid I would find out from Grandfather?' she asked softly.

Pierce took her hand, pressing a kiss into her palm before he answered. 'I was hoping you would, but I knew you wouldn't. Petrakos would never have told you.'

'But why didn't you tell me when we met again?'

He shrugged. 'I had my pride too, Alix. I knew I had done my work too well, and even I could not lay myself open to a woman who hated me. So I never told you that I couldn't live with the thought of having bartered you. I went back and forced your grandfather to accept full payment. Not that he fought me. By my return he realised how I felt about you, and he used it to get as much from me as he could. Neither did I fight him. You were worth every penny, even if you never knew it.'

She shook her head sadly. 'So you really did pay a high price for them.'

To her surprise his hand tightened about hers. 'Not money, Alix. The price I paid for the ships was you...the most precious of all my possessions. I only gave you up because I knew that I would never rest until I'd done all that I could to get you back again.'

Swallowing hard against a rising lump of emotion, Alix placed her free hand on his shirt over his heart, feeling the steady thud of life there. Felt, too, the way the beat altered at her touch. 'Pierce, don't you realise you've just laid your pride at my feet? I could walk over it just the way you invited me to.'

'You would have every right to. I've offered you my heart and my life, but if it's my pride you want, then it's yours.'

She licked her lips with studied care. 'I think . . . that it would do me no good not to forgive you, because you cannot forgive yourself. Yet I can't do anything else but forgive you, because I love you. I never really stopped loving you. So, my darling, if you love me as you say you do, you must forgive yourself too. That's what I demand of you.'

The world suddenly seemed to have gone still around them, and Alix looked bravely into eyes which blazed with a violence of emotion she had so longed to see. 'And if I can't, sweet Alix?'

'Then I'll just have to love you a whole lot more until you can,' she promised, and her words ended on a gasp as Pierce pulled her into his arms, folding them tightly round her as if he would never let her go. But she didn't mind. At last, at long, long last they were back together where they belonged, and she clung to him. They had come through a fire not of their choosing, and now they were free to look ahead of them and not behind.

'You're shaking,' Pierce breathed against her neck, and she laughed huskily.

'So are you.' She could feel the tremors going through him.

Easing back, Pierce framed her head with hands which were not quite steady. 'I thought I had lost you for good this time,' he confessed, pressing kisses over her eyes and cheeks until he reached her mouth, staying tantalisingly a breath away.

A tiny groan escaped her as she was forced to wait for the kiss she longed for. 'I would have come back, if only to punch you on the nose!'

Pierce laughed, that supreme self-confidence returning by leaps and bounds. 'You little firebrand! It's quite a thought, but I'd rather you kissed me instead.'

His teasing made her eyes flash. 'Are you begging me, Pierce?'

'So you still want your pound of flesh after all?'

She arched a look at him from beneath her lashes. 'Actually, I want about a hundred and seventy pounds of flesh quite desperately! What are you waiting for?'

'Hell, I'm actually almost afraid to touch you,' he revealed amazingly, even though his eyes sent a far different message.

In return, her own gaze flirted invitingly. 'But not so afraid you'll let me go?'

At that he laughed, and swung her up in his arms with a mastery which thrilled her. 'I'll never let you go. I'm your fate, Alix. Does that scare you?' he challenged, carrying her through to the bedroom, letting her slide to the floor by the bed, but keeping her firmly within his grasp.

Her hands glided up around his neck, fingers locking into his thick dark hair. 'Nothing scares me when I'm with you,' she confessed, and closed her eyes as his head lowered and his lips finally took hers.

It was not a kiss of passion, but of love. A promise without words which told the depths and heights of their feelings for each other. Yet in their love for each other their emotions had never been temperate, and soon that kiss was not enough. The tempo changed with their heartbeats as they sought a response that only the other could give. The kisses became longer, deeper, searching out with tongues and lips, a fire which sent a fever to the blood and left them breathless.

Clothes were discarded haphazardly, and then they were lying together on the bed, their flesh the brush of silk on velvet. Each caress scorched them, raising the temperature until their bodies were slick. They moved together, gasps of delight mixing with moans of pleasure. As her hands sought out the planes of his back and shoulders, stroking the taut line of his buttocks, Alix knew their lovemaking had never been like this before. When Pierce raised his head from her breast, the tight lines etched into his face told the tale of how hard a task it was for him to keep in control.

She was fast losing hers, and didn't care. She writhed against him as his hand sought the moist centre of her, and she melted into his stroking caress, gasping as her body arched helplessly. Then reason vanished as his mouth returned to the thrusting, aching point of her breasts, but only to pass on to the silken plane of her stomach, and lower, until he claimed her with the most intimate caress of all. Head thrashing from side to side, she cried out as her body responded with a series of delicious contractions.

Pierce moved above her again as she lay panting. He had wanted to give her pleasure, and he had, but she wanted to please him, too. Her hands went to his chest, finding the flat male nipples, teasing them with her nails until he groaned aloud, collapsing on to his back beside her. She followed him, her tongue tracing the same line, her hands foraging lower, finding and closing about the taut male shaft.

But that was all Pierce could take. His magnificent control shattered, and he took charge, rolling over until she was beneath him once more, taking possession with a driving thrust that hurtled them both towards the final

edge. Caught in the spiral, Alix welcomed the ever-
deepening thrusts until she thought she could take no
more without going mad. Then the world disintegrated
about her as she hurtled way up and out, hearing Pierce's
guttural cry as he joined her.

It was a very long time before the real world impinged
on them again. Then, with a sigh, Pierce eased himself
on to his side and propped himself up on his elbow to
gaze down at her. Alix was swimming in a sea of lethargy,
so replete that she didn't want to move, yet she opened
her eyes when he ran his fingers over her lips.

'Remind me to send you away more often, if this is
the way you welcome me back,' he teased gently,
brushing damp tendrils of hair from her cheeks.

Momentarily her eyes clouded. 'Don't you ever do that
to me again, Pierce.'

He grimaced. 'I admit I was wrong, but it's how you
make me feel. It's as if I'm so afraid of losing you, I
have to drive you away! Forgive me?'

So long as she knew he loved her, she'd forgive him
anything. 'I think I've proved it isn't that easy to get rid
of me,' she told him softly, and he groaned.

'I suppose I can't believe my luck. I keep pinching
myself to make sure it's real,' he confessed huskily,
brushing a kiss over her forehead. 'Happy?'

'Incredibly happy,' she sighed. Pierce might be able
to inflict the worst hurt, but only he could ever make
her as happy as this. They were the two sides of the coin
of loving.

Still breathing heavily, he gazed long into her eyes.
'And you do believe I love you? That despite what I did
I always have?'

Sighing again, Alix took his hand and cradled it to her cheek. 'Oh, yes. It's the only explanation which makes sense.' Her eyes lit up with an iridescent smile. 'I'm glad I don't have to hate you any longer. It's hard to do when you really love someone. Pierce, is it truly all over now?'

He nodded solemnly. 'All I want to do now is forget it. I bear no resentment towards your family. I was simply keeping a promise. From now, all my promises are for you and our own family.'

Alix pulled his arm around her, hugging it close. 'Family. That sounds nice,' she murmured, and his lips softened into a smile.

'Do I take it that means you'll no longer be wishing I come back as something nasty you can crush under your foot?'

She laughed. 'Did I really say that?'

'You did, and much more besides,' he growled in mock-anger.

'Well, you deserved it at the time,' she teased, only to sober when other thoughts impinged. 'You said some things too. The day you took me to see my grandfather you reminded me you'd never said you loved me, not in so many words.'

Pierce sobered too. 'I knew that I could never say the words and refute them later. So I told you you could never know the depth of feeling I had in my heart for you. You were meant to take that as a desire for revenge, but it was always what you first thought. That depth of feeling was love, Alix, but I had to pretend otherwise.'

So she hadn't really been wrong at all. It was good to know that, even now. Yet there was still something that hurt her deeply. 'Why did you make love to me on our wedding night? Was it really necessary to close the loophole in that way?' she asked, not realising the depth of hurt she revealed in her voice.

Pierce heard, though, and closed his eyes at the pain. 'There was never a loophole. I didn't have to make love to you, I *needed* to. It was necessary to me, my love, because I thought it might be the only time I would ever have you, the only time I could show you just how much I loved you. I wanted it to be good for you, and although I knew it would only hurt us both later I couldn't help myself. If I was going to live in hell, then I had to taste heaven just once.'

Alix gazed up at him, hating to see the way her question had forced him in on himself. Stricken, she touched her hand to his lips, and instantly he was back with her.

'It was heaven for me too, Pierce. It's always been heaven with you.'

He shook his head. 'Not always heaven, darling Alix. I know I've hurt you badly, but I intend to make up for every second of pain.'

She smiled softly, nestling up to him. 'Oh, how do you plan to do that?' she teased, trailing her fingers through the hair on his chest and tugging gently.

He winced, but didn't stop her. 'Give me a couple more minutes and I'll think of something,' he retorted huskily, and she moved against him, her thigh rubbing his.

'A few minutes?' she challenged, and gasped as he suddenly rolled over and pinned her beneath him.

'Alix Martineau, have you no shame?' he growled in mock-anger, though his eyes sent a different message, one she answered.

'I have a pain here, Pierce,' she sighed, pointing to her lips. 'Won't you kiss it and make it better?'

His eyes glittered, and he lowered his head, taking her mouth in a searing kiss. 'Better?' he queried huskily.

Her arms crept up around his neck. 'Try again; I'll tell you when to stop,' she invited, and with a throaty laugh he obliged.

HARLEQUIN PRESENTS®

The heat wave continues...

Watch out for our scorching selection of stories...

They're

Coming next month:

Making Magic by Karen van der Zee

Harlequin Presents #1729

Trouble in Paradise?

Max Laurello was busy writing his next bestseller under Caribbean-blue skies, and he had no time for "demanding, meddlesome, infuriating females"! Well, he didn't have to worry on Katrina's account. She had come to the coconut-palmed white beaches of St. Barlow to pick up the pieces of her life. After a disastrous marriage to the philandering Bastian, the last thing she intended to do was let the sun go to her head and fall for a womanizer like Max!

Available in March wherever Harlequin books are sold.

THTH-2-R

HARLEQUIN®

Deceit, betrayal, murder

Join Harlequin's intrepid heroines, India Leigh
and Mary Hadfield, as they ferret out the truth
behind the mysterious goings-on in their
neighborhood. These two women are no milk-
and-water misses. In fact, they thrive on

Watch for their incredible adventures in this
special two-book collection. Available in March,
wherever Harlequin books are sold.

HARLEQUIN®

PRESENTS Plus

Lindsey and Tim Ramsden were married—but, these days, in name only. Their once-passionate relationship hadn't survived a bitter misunderstanding, and they were separated by time and the Atlantic Ocean. Now Lindsey had another chance at happiness; could she accept that her marriage was finally over, and that it was time to move on?

"The first man to walk through this door will be the one I date for a month...." And he turned out to be Leo Kozakis—the man who had cruelly rejected Jacy ten years before! The sensible thing would be to forget the wager, but Jacy was seized by another reckless impulse: she was more than a match now for Leo—and she would seize her chances for passion...and revenge!

Presents Plus is Passion Plus!

Coming next month:

The Wrong Kind of Wife by Roberta Leigh
Harlequin Presents Plus #1725

and

Gamble on Passion by Jacqueline Baird
Harlequin Presents Plus #1726

Harlequin Presents Plus
The best has just gotten better!

Available in March wherever Harlequin books are sold.

PPLUS22-R

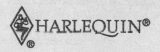

HARLEQUIN®

Don't miss these Harlequin favorites by some of our most
distinguished authors!
And now, you can receive a discount by ordering two or more titles!

HT#25577	WILD LIKE THE WIND by Janice Kaiser	$2.99	☐
HT#25589	THE RETURN OF CAINE O'HALLORAN by JoAnn Ross	$2.99	☐
HP#11626	THE SEDUCTION STAKES by Lindsay Armstrong	$2.99	☐
HP#11647	GIVE A MAN A BAD NAME by Roberta Leigh	$2.99	☐
HR#03293	THE MAN WHO CAME FOR CHRISTMAS by Bethany Campbell	$2.89	☐
HR#03308	RELATIVE VALUES by Jessica Steele	$2.89	☐
SR#70589	CANDY KISSES by Muriel Jensen	$3.50	☐
SR#70598	WEDDING INVITATION by Marisa Carroll	$3.50 U.S. $3.99 CAN.	☐ ☐
HI#22230	CACHE POOR by Margaret St. George	$2.99	☐
HAR#16515	NO ROOM AT THE INN by Linda Randall Wisdom	$3.50	☐
HAR#16520	THE ADVENTURESS by M.J. Rodgers	$3.50	☐
HS#28795	PIECES OF SKY by Marianne Willman	$3.99	☐
HS#28824	A WARRIOR'S WAY by Margaret Moore	$3.99 U.S. $4.50 CAN.	☐ ☐

(limited quantities available on certain titles)

	AMOUNT	$
DEDUCT:	**10% DISCOUNT FOR 2+ BOOKS**	$
ADD:	**POSTAGE & HANDLING**	$
	($1.00 for one book, 50¢ for each additional)	
	APPLICABLE TAXES*	$_____
	TOTAL PAYABLE	$_____
	(check or money order—please do not send cash)	

To order, complete this form and send it, along with a check or money order for the
total above, payable to Harlequin Books, to: **In the U.S.:** 3010 Walden Avenue,
P.O. Box 9047, Buffalo, NY 14269-9047; **In Canada:** P.O. Box 613, Fort Erie, Ontario,
L2A 5X3.

Name: _____

Address: _____ City: _____

State/Prov.: _____ Zip/Postal Code: _____

*New York residents remit applicable sales taxes.
Canadian residents remit applicable GST and provincial taxes.

HBACK-JM2